ELIZABETH, GUARDIAN OF DRAGONS

A REVERSE HAREM PARANORMAL ROMANCE

AVA MASON

To my readers
Because of you, my whole existence is validated

*K*nee bouncing, I pulled at the string attached to the bottom of my dress and wrestled with my inner demons. I'd saved a woman who despised me, beat me to the ground and rubbed my face in her filth. And yet, I couldn't save the man I loved.

The Queen's words tumbled over the table, doing cartwheels and flips, trying to garner my attention. But my thoughts were on her words from a different day.

It had only been three days, but they felt like a lifetime ago.

I made a promise and immediately failed. To her. To my clan. To my guys.

I'd promised to lead and guide them. To protect them.

Protect.

Air whistled through my teeth as the silent word on my tongue made it feel thick and foreign. It was loaded with promise and assurance. To protect him with my dying breath.

And I couldn't even keep it once.

Avery still refused to speak, or to consider staying with the team. My clan was feeling angry, sad, and lost. And a little bit impatient.

I looked down, realizing that I'd yanked the string on my dress so hard that I had pulled out the hem.

I heard Easton's name and my head snapped up. "Huh?"

Eyebrow raised, the Queen answered. "I thought that would get your attention."

I rubbed my face. "I'm sorry." Ignoring the royal figure in front of me was very rude. And probably deadly.

She rubbed her fingers across her lips, studying me. We were sitting at a table in her suite. Like for reals, I was actually in the Queen's section of the castle, a place where I imagined she practically invited no one. Except for Gerard, of course. And the fifty other soldiers that guarded the wing. And James. And probably a long trail of lovers. And maybe the rest of her family, if she had any.

So. Yeah. Anyway. I was here and I guess that made me special. Did I really want to be all that special? No, I did not.

I looked around, noting that her office was lined with old and presumptuous looking books. I'd seen a couple of titles when I'd arrived. Shit, like, Theory of Nuclear Magnetic Resonance, and, Power, Order, Violence and Justice. I even saw what appeared to be an original copy of Moby Dick and wondered if she'd actually read that thing. If she'd actually read any of those crazy ass titled books.

My eyes drifted to the door attached to her office and I mused about what could be beyond this room.

Was it her bedroom? Did she ever bring guys back here? Did she bring them through this office first to impress them with her smart books, then drag them back to some enormously soft bed to make passionate love? I eyed her body. Not that she would have to drag any guy anywhere. She probably had a million dudes lined up to pretend to be interested in nuclear magnetic resonance just to see that tight bod under her fancy clothes.

How many lovers did she have?

I pinched my leg. I had no fucking right to wonder about that.

Her sigh caught my attention again and I looked up, my cheeks blushing. I was doing a horrible job of even pretending that I was listening.

She stood up and began to walk towards the door I'd been eyeing earlier. "Come with me, Elizabeth."

Oh no. She'd called me Elizabeth. Was I in trouble?

Standing up, I walked behind her, just a step. I wasn't sure what protocol was when walking with the Queen, even though she'd declared me a sister of sorts. My upbringing was so impressed on me that I couldn't help but show her respect by letting her go ahead of me.

She stopped and so did I. She turned, her hands folded across her chest. She had a scowl on her face.

Bad. That was bad.

"I don't have cooties, you know."

I shrugged. "Well, I didn't know. I haven't been instructed on the inoculation of Queens." Then I forced myself to smile and grabbed her hand, tucking it through mine. "I'm sorry. I've had a shi-crappy week."

She leaned into me, just a little bit and it gave me a warm glowy feeling. Were we becoming friends?

"Tell me, what's going on?" Even though she was leaning onto me, giving the impression that I was in charge, she had a way of leading me in a way that was so natural, so gentle and yet, so compelling that I couldn't do anything else but lead-follow her. I wondered if she'd read how to do that in one of her fancy books or if it just came naturally to her.

I tucked my hair behind my ear. "Well, you know about the battle with Sophia. And that someone tried to kill me." Her hold on my arm tightened just slightly. "And then Avery came home from some super secret mission that no one will talk about." We were at the door now and she'd grabbed the handle. Instead of opening right away, it made a whirring noise and a red laser scanned her hand. Then, there was a click and she pulled it open. The door didn't lead to her bedroom but light filtered in from the outside and I braced myself for a blast of cold air. "And now he says he wants to..." I stared at the landscape around me. "Holy Queen Mary of Scots, Batman!"

❦

Instead of a wintry wonderland, we stepped out into the most magical garden I had ever seen in my life. It spread for acres, lined with colorful flowers and delicate trees. I thought the Botanical gardens were amazing, but this blew my mind. First of all, it wasn't even cold. There wasn't a single snowflake anywhere. Butterflies chased each other through air which smelled liked honeysuckle.

"Keep going." The sides of her lips were turned upwards, just a tiny bit, like maybe she was proud of her garden.

"And… and. What was I talking about?" I was lead-following her towards rows of purple, pink and red flowers.

"Avery."

"Oh yes." I took in a deep breath. Suddenly, the thing with Avery didn't seem like something I should be sharing. It felt too personal somehow. Besides, she had much bigger problems than my love life. "I'm sorry. What was it you were trying to tell me?"

She paused for a moment, a look of concern on her face. "I'm sorry you're having such a hard time with your clan."

I wanted to protest but she stopped me.

"I know that this country, the world of dragons, is…" She spread her hand out, thinking before she settled on a word. "Different. You still have a lot to learn about the intricacies of our magic and binding power. Plus, you've been dealing with everything that has been thrown at you since the death of your parents. It's a lot to take in."

I took in a deep breath, pushing away the suffocating feeling that threatened to choke out tears.

"But you've always been an Alpha, Lizzy. You're still a leader. A strong one." The side of her lip turned up, just enough to convey her trust in me. "And I highly doubt that the warrior who took down one of the most dangerous dragons in the kingdom can't figure out how to handle her clan."

I gulped down a breath. The Queen had so much trust in me. So did all of my guys. I couldn't let them down. I pressed my lips into a firm line and shook my head. I would figure this out. I would keep the team together. Because even though Avery hadn't said the words himself in a ceremony, he was *mine*. I would show him that he still belonged, that he was still loved and needed, no matter what had happened.

"What did my dad do?"

The question spilled from my lips from nowhere, surprising even me, and yet, it was the question that had pressed at the back of my mind since I'd met the guys. Her eyes widened and she turned away, but pulled me deeper into her garden.

"There wasn't one thing in particular that your father did. It was anything and everything that he did. In the way that he looked at you, as if you were the most important thing in the world. He demanded your respect but gave it in return. He would do anything you asked, as long as it didn't go against his moral code. Also, there were some rumors that he had taken down some ruthless killers." She looked at me. "Wolves."

I sucked in a breath. That he would take out wolves in favor of the dragons would be seen as a betrayal among the pack.

"Except he would never admit to it." She smiled, touching her lips, as if remembering something. "His love of chocolate was probably the only thing that could rival his modesty."

I grinned. He loved chocolate as much as I did.

She shrugged. "He had a particular way of bringing out the best in you. He made you want to earn his respect, for him to be proud of you."

I nodded, knowing exactly what she meant. The sun's golden rays warmed my skin and I wanted to throw off my dress and run around in it. I was beginning to tire of the snow and was happy that the spring was coming soon. I opened my hand as if I could catch the rays in my hand and rub it over me like lotion.

I sighed. "Did you ever date my dad?"

She burst out laughing, jerking out of my arm to lean over.

"Gah, what the hell? Why is that so funny?" I raised my eyebrow at her, unamused, even though her laugher was musical and welcoming.

Holding her hand to her chest, she took in a deep breath. She grappled at me, looking for my arm again and I pulled her up. Her smile was bright and carefree and I wished I could see it more often. The

Queen lived life to the fullest. Whether it was in happiness or serious-ness, she did it all the way.

"Heavens, no. I had a little bit of a crush at first, of course. All the girls at University did. But it didn't matter. I wasn't allowed to date anyone, not just him." She waved her hand. "Anyway, once he met your mother, his eyes were for her and her alone. He never even looked at anyone else after that." A shadow passed over her face. She grew serious and I knew that talk of my dad was over. "Elizabeth, you know that the magic of my Kingdom, *my* magic, is tied to the artifacts. You also know that I suspect Andre has been collecting them."

I nodded.

She waved her arm around us. "This garden is something I created as a child."

Holy crap. My mouth dropped open. "You were a kid when you did this?" And I thought my childhood was magical.

"I was about three when it started growing. It just suddenly happened. I didn't mean to do it, but my magic just spilled over." She held her finger out and a butterfly landed on it. I stared at it in wonder. "Of course, it wasn't as big as this. It was only a few flowers. But as my magic grew, so did the garden."

Suddenly the garden came alive around me, the buzzing of bees was louder and the flowers swayed, basking in the sun. It was if it wanted to show off the beauty of its owner.

"For as long as I've lived, I've maintained this garden effortlessly." She frowned. "But lately, the flowers have begun to die. And it's becoming harder and harder to keep up. I used to do it naturally, without any effort. But now, I have to think about it to maintain it." Her face was sad; she couldn't bear this fact. Something that had clung to her very existence, her childhood, was fading away.

We were headed towards the edge of the garden and I realized that several rows of flowers were in different stages of dying. Even some of the delicate trees bowed over, as if in pain. She turned to look into my face. "I share this garden with only those in whom I have ultimate trust."

Suddenly my throat was dry and I knew that she'd brought me

here for a reason. Of course, she'd probably already asked my help but I wasn't listening earlier. I tried to make up for it. "What can I do to help?"

She bit her lip, considering my words. "I need a spy. Someone to watch Andre for me."

I nodded, considering her words. "And you think one of my guys can help you?"

She stopped, pausing, and it made her next words heavy. "Actually, I need Sophia to do it."

I choked on my spit. "What?"

"You're her Alpha now. She must obey you."

"Yeah, but it's not like I have any plans to order her around. Especially to spy on her own boss."

"Andre is more than a boss to her. He's raised her since her father died."

I sucked in a breath. Holy shit, seriously? "And you want me to tell her to spy on her surrogate father?"

"She's perfectly positioned to watch him. You are her Alpha now. What did you think this meant? That you'd be able to avoid her forever?"

"No, but I thought I'd just run interference between her and the guys. Let her live her life as normal, otherwise."

She frowned. "That would be very... disappointing. I had much higher hopes for you."

Scowling, I walked deeper into the garden, leaving her behind. I studied the intricate patterns of the garden, noting that some of the flowers were so complicated, they probably were unique in the world. It wasn't necessarily that I was afraid of Sophia, or averse to telling her what to do. It was the opposite. I was afraid of myself around her. Could I keep my anger in check?

The smell of a rabbit passed through my nose and the hair on the back of my neck stood on end. Oh what fun this little wolf could have in this garden. I turned back towards her.

"I'm assuming you need information as to exactly where Andre is keeping the artifacts."

She shrugged. "If it is Andre. Right now, it's only a suspicion. It's hard to watch him because he's in charge of my Special Ops. Plus, he's very careful. If it is him, we need to know whether he is destroying the artifacts or hiding them for his own reasons. If he's hiding them, he's suppressing their power somehow."

I nodded, eyeing the dying rows of flowers. "Ok, I'll ask her. Or command her to do it. Whichever is necessary."

She smiled. "I knew I could count on you." She hesitated a moment, biting her lip. "There is something else. Somehow Andre found out that we were meeting. He has requested a meeting with you also."

I frowned. "Why?"

She shrugged. "He said something about a missing file."

I sucked in a breath. Damn. I waved her off. "I'll meet with him another day." That was definitely a meeting I could put off. Forever, if possible.

"Actually, that's part of what I need from you. Maybe you can turn the tables on him. Get some information from him. In fact, I need you to meet with him."

I sighed. Of course. Being a sister to the Queen was never going to be easy. I grinned. "Yes, my Queen."

Scowling, she took my arm and we began to walk back towards her office. "If you don't stop calling me Queen in private, I'll have to put a magic spell over you." She eyed my hair. "I heard that Christian prefers your hair pink."

I sucked in a breath and put a hand to my head. "You wouldn't dare."

"I would." She spoke with such certainty, I had no doubts that she would.

"Fine, Aria."

"Oh!" She grinned. "I didn't realize how nice that would feel."

Smiling, I reached the door and stopped. Holding her arm and looking into her earnest eyes, her walls were down again and they radiated sincerity. And then I wondered if she had any lovers at all. Or friends. There was something about her, just like my dad, that made me fiercely protective of her. I wanted her respect. "Quee— Aria." I was too used to calling her The Queen. As in THE Queen. It would take a while to get used to calling her anything else. She was the only Queen I knew, after all. "I'm prepared to do whatever you need. Just say the word."

She studied my face. "There is something else I need. But I'm not sure if you're the right person to ask."

I frowned. "Well, if it has to do with the artifacts, I have a suspicion that my team may be up to the task. Despite any deficiency I bring."

She frowned. "Don't underestimate yourself, Lizzy. You're just now coming into your powers. And you just defeated one of the most powerful shifters I know. And I'm not talking about Sophia."

I raised my eyebrow. "Huh?" Did one say 'huh' to a Queen? And who had I defeated, if it wasn't Sophia?

She pointed at my chest. "Yourself."

I sucked in a breath. "How do you...?"

"I am not an idiot. I know everything and everyone. I knew the power that ring held when I gave it to you. I warned you. I told you it was powerful." She tilted her head. "And you chose mercy instead of vengeance. That says a lot about you. You're just like your dad."

I sucked in a breath and my nose tingled with unspent tears. That was the highest compliment anyone had ever paid me, and my body hummed with her praise.

She nodded. "There are two artifacts I need. One is out in the open for anyone to see. I need you to trade it for a look-alike so that no one will know it is gone. If I take it out in the open, then Andre will know and may push his plans forward."

I nodded. "Consider it done."

"The other one, I need it taken quietly and kept safe. A thief will have to take it, not an army. And you're not going to like where it's stored."

"Absolutely." I took in a deep breath. "Just tell me what I need to do."

She smiled and it almost reached her eyes. "I have everything you will need inside. And Liam will be your point of contact. If anything goes wrong, anything at all, he will be the one you call."

I nodded. Her hand was on the door but she didn't open it, her thumb fiddled with the latch. She was trying to decide if she was going to tell me something. "During the Alpha ceremony, you know that you marked James as yours, right?"

§

WHAT. THE. ACTUAL. FUCK.

I was driving home now, reeling from Queen Aria's revelation.

What the hell was wrong with me? Didn't I have enough men on my plate? Not to mention the fact that James was seriously pissed at me right now.

My mind went to the night before my fight with Sophia and the way his hands touched mine. And that vulnerable look on his face when he'd told me about his sister... My hands trembled on the steering wheel. He fucking trusted me. And then I let him down. Now I knew that it was him who was mad at me at the Alpha ceremony. When everyone's feelings came rushing in and I'd felt anger.

That was him. I had no doubt.

And yet, I couldn't deny that the thought of him made me shiver. I pretended like he didn't do things to me. Apparently my wolf, or whatever the 'F' it was, didn't care that I was pretending. That bitch just took whoever the hell she wanted and didn't care that four fucking men was enough for one woman.

I careened around the corner a little too fast. The snow was finally beginning to melt, making the roads slippery. I downshifted to force myself to slow down; I didn't want to wreck Easton's car. He'd probably kill me. I took in a deep breath and suddenly thoughts of my parents filled my mind. Talking about my dad had brought up the pain of their death. I realized that every attempt to suppress thoughts of home were slowly leaking back through my walls. I took in another deep breath to face reality. I missed it.

I wanted to go back. To save my pack. To be home again.

But as much as I wanted to go home, I was also afraid to do it. To see my parents' house empty and destroyed; the stains from my parents' blood, it would destroy me. I sucked in a breath. Just the thought of it made tears splotch my eyes, clouding my vision. I didn't know if I was brave enough to face that right now. I wasn't sure that was something I would ever be ready to face.

So even though I wanted to return home, I could put it off. For now.

I'd help the Queen. Aria. I'd help her; she trusted me and I could do this for her.

And, I'd find a way to release my hold on James. Just because I'd marked him, didn't mean I had to have him. I wouldn't force this on him. I would find a way to free him, to break the bond.

The voice from the GPS interrupted my thoughts and I skidded as I made the next turn. A horn blared from behind me and I opened my window. "My bad!"

Shit. I needed to get myself together before I wrecked and hurt someone. I slowed down and pulled to a stop into the closest parking lot.

Something was wrong with Avery.

Someone was trying to kill me.

Someone was trying to overthrow Aria.

I had to make Sophia spy on her surrogate father and not lose my shit around her.

I have to go home and kick Garrett's ass.

Shit. Everything was coming to a head all at once.

I pulled out my phone, staring at it. Old habits were hard to break. Every time I was overwhelmed, I wanted to call Aaron.

My fingers punched the number that was as familiar as my parent's number. As my own. A number that I'd seen hundreds of times. I didn't hit send.

Was I really going to do this?

Hunter showed me how to make my number untraceable but that didn't mean that there would be no consequences from this act. I could put myself in serious danger. The question was, did I trust him?

I thought of Aaron crawling his way towards me, sacrificing himself and his dignity for me. How he tried to save me. He, alone, stared down two packs of wolves.

I hit enter, wiping at my cheeks.

The phone rang once, twice. My stomach twisted in knots.

"Hello?"

I inhaled a sharp breath. God, it felt so good to hear his voice.

"Hello?"

I couldn't answer. I couldn't breathe.

"Lizzy?" His voice. It sounded so... hopeful. And so... broken.

Panicking, I hit the 'end' button and threw my phone to the other side of the car, like it was on fire and would burn me up. Could it... Did he...

Did he marry Olivia? I didn't know for sure, did I? I'd taken Shayne at his word. I didn't believe that Shayne would lie to me but maybe... maybe Aaron defied his father. Maybe he rebelled.

I rubbed my face. Shit. I needed to know for sure.

Frowning, I reached across the car to grab my phone again. I had things I needed to do first, to fix.

Number one: Avery.

He was my top priority. I took in a deep breath. He wasn't going to be an easy fix but it didn't matter. He was worth whatever hell he dragged me through; I'd do whatever it took to get him back.

I put the car back in drive and pulled out onto the road, a little calmer, and dialed Easton.

Number two: put my clan together and get shit done.

ॐ

WHEN I PULLED UP THE DRIVEWAY, EASTON WAS OUTSIDE, WAITING FOR me. I couldn't stop the grin that spread out on my face. Damn if he didn't heal my heart a little bit each time I saw him. He jogged to the car, his footsteps light on the melting snow, and opened my door. A blast of love overwhelmed me and I looked up to his smiling face. It was exactly what I needed right now.

"Hi." His white t-shirt gripped his muscled chest and his jeans clung to his hips.

"Hi." I couldn't stop thinking of our night together, the way his sexy body wrapped me up in kisses and commands.

He pulled me out of the car and folded his arms around me. I stared into his dark brown eyes, a blush marking my cheeks as his finger traced them.

"I called Sophia; she should be here soon."

"Good." My hand fell to his chest and he stepped forward, pushing me against his car and trapping my hand between us. His lips touched the top of my head and he rubbed across it, causing a burning heat to shoot to my chest. Then his mouth moved to my ear, his voice, dark and delicious, tickled my skin.

"Do you feel what you do to me, Lizzy?" He pressed his hardness against me. "Right now I want to tell you to drop to your knees and take care of my problem."

Shit. That voice. The way it made me tremble. "Yes."

His hands roamed up my side and I pressed myself into him. Willing the world around us to end, wishing we didn't have a mission to complete. His fingers burned through the thin material of my dress and I was putty in his hands. Then his fingers crossed the span of my back and he tugged the back of my hair, forcing my head back to look into his face. His eyes were dark and smoldering.

I groaned and the temptation to fall at his feet was so strong, that I almost did it. Fuck the icy slush, fuck that we were out in the open and fuck all my problems. I wanted Easton right here, right now.

But his fingers caught at my elbow and I leaned into him so that he was supporting me.

"Next time I see you in that sexy dress, I'm going to make you kneel at my feet and beg me to put my thick cock in that pouty mouth of yours." I shivered. "I'm going to touch you in all your secret places so inappropriately that you'll beg me to never let you go."

I nipped at his shoulder and his grip on my hair tightened. We stood like that for a moment, just staring into each others eyes, unwilling to look away. And then he glanced behind me and, for a second I thought that Sophia was pulling up. He nodded at someone passing by and suddenly the spell between us broke.

He reached his hand down to fix himself and I closed my eyes, reigning in my emotions. I had to be a leader and not be jerked around by my hormones. Sighing, he took a step back and I let him create distance between us. Now wasn't the time. I bit my lip harshly, bringing me back to face my task.

I took in a deep breath and bent back down to grab my bag from the Queen out of the passenger seat. I handed it to him. "Has anything changed?"

He turned his face to the side, looking towards the house. "Nothing new. Christian's in there with him now."

"Alright," I turned my body towards the house determinedly. "Let's get ready."

*a*s soon as I opened the door, Christian's loud voice broke through my thoughts. "You have to tell her what happened. It's the only way to fix this."

Avery growled in response. "I'm leaving. You won't change my mind."

"You can't leave her; she has a right to know. And you can't just abandon the team." Something shattered.

Avery's voice was sarcastic. "Oh, nice. Real mature. And you say I'm the one throwing a hissy fit."

Easton and I rushed into Avery's room. The emotion level in the house was so high, that I was surprised it hadn't exploded. I looked at Christian, eyeing the broken lamp. "What's going on?"

He sat down on Avery's bed, right on top of Avery's bag that he was trying to pack. We'd held him off for two days, but apparently he'd decided he wouldn't wait any longer.

"Avery has to talk to you about something." Christian didn't look as angry as I thought he would be.

But Avery - his face was lit with rage. "You have no idea what you're talking about, even if you think you do. But it doesn't matter. I don't have time for this; I have to get out of here." He tried to yank his bag out from under Christian, who grabbed it tight. Avery yanked it off the bed, pulling Christian with him.

"Let go." Avery dragged Christian across the room, who looked at me, grinning. I held in the laugh that threatened to spill from my lips.

After pulling him almost into his closet, Avery dropped the handle.

"I don't care about the bag anyway. I'll just buy what I need." He looked up at Easton and me and I knew he wanted to bolt for the door. But we were standing in his way.

Then the doorbell rang and I jumped. "Sophia."

I was looking at Avery when I said it and his face grew a deep red. He ran towards the door, pushing me and Easton out of the way with such force that we grabbed at the frame, surprised. Then we all rushed out after him.

His footsteps across the wooden floor were surprisingly light and he yanked the door open. Sophia's face changed from a scowl into shock as soon as she saw Avery. He blocked her from entering. "No."

She was wearing jeans and a sweatshirt, with her hair piled on her head. There were deep, dark lines under her bloodshot eyes. She looked horrible. Every ounce of anger I had towards her melted at the harrowed look on her face.

She frowned. "She asked me to come here."

Suddenly, Avery emitted a loud, strangling noise. He grabbed Sophia's shirt and yanked her forward. She cried out as he turned and slammed her against the wall. "You fucking bitch, I can't believe you did that to me!"

Her mouth dropped and she pulled at his hands which were clinched in her sweatshirt.

His wings popped out from his back, tearing his shirt as his dragon magic spilled out into the room.

Sophia's mascara was smeared across her face. Had she been crying? "I swear I didn't know. I swear it!"

He was in her face now, his features scrunched up in anger. Scales rippled across his skin; he was losing control. "How could you not know? It's your fucking job! It's your fucking job to know every little thing." He shook his head. "No. You knew. You knew it!" Suddenly his magic exploded, pushing Easton, Christian and I across the room. Christian wrapped his arms around me, breaking my fall.

Easton groaned from his spot on the floor. "Dammit, Avery."

"Give me one reason not to rip your head from your body." Avery wasn't yelling anymore, but his voice had grown low, dangerous. Threatening. Deadly.

Growling, she threw out her own dragon magic and it slammed against him. He kept a tight hold on her sweatshirt and they flew across the room, landing to the floor together. They grappled for control and she landed on top.

"I told you, I didn't know. There are people who were given permission and I had no idea what the hell was going on. I just followed orders." She leaned forward, and her nose touched his. "Just like you did."

He growled. "You had no problem disobeying orders when it came to Hunter."

She gasped, then her face became a mask of rage. She punched him in the face. Avery's mouth dropped open and his hands loosened on her sweatshirt. Then she was hitting him, over and over, in an uncontrolled frenzy of anger. I scrambled to my feet and Christian pushed on my butt to help me up.

"Sophia!"

Avery didn't stop her, didn't move to block her blows. He just let her hit him.

Her rings cut his face and blood sprayed across her shirt when she broke his nose. But she didn't stop, even after his blood was all over her, even though he lay there, not even blocking her blows. She kept hitting him, screaming an unintelligible mix of words and cusses.

"Sophia, stop!" It was a command and she stopped mid-air. Then her face crumpled and she fell into Avery's arms, crying. Avery pushed her off him and scrambled to his feet.

"I'm not falling for that."

She didn't stop crying but balled up on the floor, moving her arm across her to cover her face. Easton pulled Christian to his feet and I ran towards them. Staring down at Sophia, I rubbed my face. Holy shite, what the hell was going on?

"Sophia." I bent over, my voice soft.

"No." Her hand flew out, stopping me, and her voice held a warning.

I looked up at Avery, frowning. He was looming over her, breathing heavily. His hands were balled up in fists and he was looking at her like he wanted to hit her.

"Avery." My voice was sharp. He looked at me and his face softened when he saw me.

"I wasn't... I wouldn't..." He couldn't finish.

Then a shadow filled the doorway and we all looked up. Hunter was standing there and damn if he wasn't glorious. It was the first time I'd seen him since the Alpha fight; they'd taken him back to the hospital.

He frowned, looking over the room. The furniture had been pushed in all directions and several books had fallen off the shelves. All the pictures on the wall were crooked, hanging haphazardly. One of the framed pictures had fallen to the floor; a cracked selfie of the team, grinning like crazyheads, stared up at us.

"What's going on?" Hunter looked at me.

Avery grabbed his keys; dried blood caked his shirt, and stark blue bruises made his face look hollow. He still hadn't shaven and his beard gave him a ragged look. "None of your business." He began to walk towards the door. "Get out of my way."

Hunter frowned, crossed his arms and leaned against the door-jamb. He wasn't completely blocking it, but he also looked like he would if Avery tried to brush past him. "Really?"

"Avery." I had to make him stay, stop him from leaving.

Ignoring me, Avery paused at the door to give Hunter a hard glare. Hunter met his eyes and he didn't move out of Avery's way.

I began to feel desperate. Avery couldn't leave. Not now. Panic rose in my chest, threatening to choke my air. If he left now, would I ever see him again? "Don't leave. Please. Not like this. Not after this."

Avery stilled, but kept staring at Hunter. For some reason he didn't brush past him. I growled, knowing I would do whatever it took to keep him here.

"Don't make me use my Alpha on you."

His head snapped towards me. "You wouldn't."

I folded my arms across my chest. "Try me."

He scowled, then turned around and threw his keys on the console table. "Fine." He looked up at me as he stepped over Sophia, who was still on the floor, and walked towards his room. "But I'm leaving by tonight."

I sighed and Christian's soft fingers were on my arm. It tingled and then there was a shot of warmth through me. He was my very own little calming machine. I needed to figure out a way to just insert him into my chest. Want to kill me? No problem. I'm a calm motherpucker who can do anything.

"Sophia." Hunter bent over her. "Are you okay?"

She wouldn't look at him.

Christian went to her side. "Look, everything will work itself out, I'm sure."

She closed her eyes, ignoring them.

I brushed my hand through my hair then looked at Easton. He gave me a reassuring smile.

I took in a deep breath and waved my hands at the disheveled room. "Easton and Christian, can you put the room back together?" They nodded. "Hunter, go talk to Avery. Maybe you can talk some sense into him. Sophia, I need you in my room, we need to talk."

"But—"

"That's not a question."

She was quiet and Hunter held his hand to her. She took it and stood up. Half of her hair was out of her hairband and she yanked the band out. Pulling it into a loose ponytail, she began to walk towards my room, not looking at me.

"Third one on the right," I called out to her.

She didn't answer and at this point, I didn't care. Christian pushed the couches back where they belonged and Hunter picked up the picture, looking at it sadly. Easton held his hand towards him and Hunter passed him the photo.

I put my hand over Hunter's. "It'll be okay. We'll work this out."

He met my eyes. "I know." His confidence washed over me like a warm blanket. He caught my face with his palm. "I missed you."

I leaned into him, loving the way he felt against me. I could feel his heart beating through his chest. It was strong and steady. That was Hunter for you.

"I missed you, too. I'm glad you're out of the hospital." They'd kept him to make sure he would recover.

He chuckled. "Ain't no hospital keeping me from you."

I grinned, then looked up into his face. He reached down and tenderly met my lips with his. His kiss was soft and probing, as if he was questioning my love for him after my time with Easton. I took his face in my hands, answering him with my kiss. My whole body felt warm and tingly, and he squeezed me tighter. I wanted to stay in his embrace forever. He let me down, breaking the kiss.

"I'll go talk to Avery. Maybe knock some sense into him if necessary." He gave me one more peck, then left.

Easton was already brushing the broken frame glass into the trash can and Christian was pushing the sofa back where it belonged. Sighing, I turned away from them and went towards my room, steeling myself.

❧

SHE DIDN'T LOOK UP WHEN I OPENED THE DOOR BUT QUICKLY WIPED AT her splotchy face. Her eyes were hollow and dark, bitter, and I couldn't help but feel her anger radiating across the room at me.

I sat on the edge of my dresser, frowning at her. I don't like people who hurt my guys. "You shouldn't have hit him."

She scowled. "He was being an asshole. What else was I supposed to do?"

"True. But does that make it right? He didn't hit you back."

"He wanted to."

I crossed my arms, raising my eyebrow. "Apparently, he's pretty pissed off at you. Do you deserve his anger?"

The room grew silent and she put her feet up on the bed, pressing her face into her knees. Finally she mumbled something.

"What? I can't hear you."

She looked up at me. "I said, he didn't tell you what happened?"

I exhaled air through my teeth. "What, Avery? Talk?"

The side of her lips twisted back up but she forced them back into a firm line. I sighed again and stood up. She gave me a strange look as I moved towards her. My blanket was a soft blue, down feather and I wanted to wrap us up in it. Or strangle her with it. One of the two.

Instead, I sat next to her on the bed, rubbing my face.

"Look, forget about that for now. What the hell is going on with you?" I eyed her feet; she was wearing soft canvas shoes. "You're not yourself."

She huffed, looking away. "I don't have to answer you."

"Actually, you do." I thought back to the arena, about the power I'd held over her. Her life literally in my hands. It felt so strange to have that power over someone, to know that this person wouldn't be sitting here if I'd made a different choice. Did she even know that she had died? That for seconds, her life had been snuffed, like a candle blown out, with only the smoke of her shitstorm left to testify that she'd even been alive. Did she have anyone who would've mourned her?

She looked at me and her eyes were cold. "I've had a really shitty couple of months okay." Her lips twisted up in a sneer and she waved her arm at me. "But you wouldn't know about that, not the princess of the team."

Her words hit me like a knife to the gut. Strangle her with the blanket, it is. Tears sprung to my eyes but I tried not to let her see them, so I growled, letting my anger show. "I know what a shitty day is like."

She looked into my eyes and I knew the exact moment she remembered about my parents. Her pained eyes mirrored my own. I looked away, biting down on my resentment.

"Look, we need to talk. Christian told me about you and my dad." I considered telling her about what else I knew about her past: her miscarriages and her own abusive father, but I decided against it. "I know you knew him." I took in a deep breath, not believing what I was about to say. "I'm sorry he died."

She inhaled a sharp breath and looked away, biting her lip.

I continued. "I know he'd like to be here for you if he could."

Suddenly, she looked at me and I ignored the tears that threatened to spill from her eyes. "Were you lying to me? In the arena. Was that a lie, just to piss me off?"

I frowned. "About what?"

"About my lineage. My name?"

I shook my head. "No."

"How do you know?"

"The question is, did you know?"

She jerked her head back like I'd slapped her. "I had no idea. I'm not even sure if I believe you."

I frowned. "Easton discovered it from his magical book after we fixed it."

She was quiet; I could see that she was biting the inside of her cheeks then she squeezed her eyes tight. "So Hunter knows?"

I sprung up and paced the space next to the bed. "Look, Sophia, you need to accept this. Hunter doesn't belong to you. He doesn't want to be with you."

"You don't think I know that?" Her voice cracked and her eyes flew open.

Damn, she was so pitiful.

I faced her, needing to drive in the point. She needed to move on, for her sake. "I'm not sure you do."

Her face contorted into a mixture of anger and shame. She sputtered. "You have no idea what I'm thinking. You have no idea who I am. You've known me for all of two-seconds. Just because you're my Alpha now, doesn't mean you can intrude in my life. Tell me who or what I am."

I leaned over, my expression fierce as a wave of possession washed over me. "Hunter is mine. He chose me. You stay the fuck away from him. Is that clear?"

She scowled but nodded.

"Okay then." I sat back down on the bed, trying to decide where to go from here and an awkward silence settled around us. I could ask her about Avery but I wanted to hear it from him. He needed to be the one to reveal what the hell was going on.

I also still needed to talk to her about her assignment but I felt like I should talk to her about what she was going through. She hadn't lied, she was having a really crappy few months. She'd lost almost everything she'd held dear: Hunter, her reputation. I had a crazy feeling that she honestly hadn't known about her lineage.

But she still had a lot to look forward to, a future. If she wanted it, she could easily have it. She just didn't realize it. And I begrudgingly admitted that I should try to help her. It's what a good Alpha would do; it's what my dad would've done. Many times he'd turned bitter, lone wolves into devoted members of the pack.

"Look, Sophia." I put my knee up on the bed, twisting to face her but she leaned away from me.

"I know you don't like me much. But I just want you to know, you can talk to me any time you want. I'm here for you." I took in a deep breath. "And you're still smoking hot. If you'd open yourself up a little, quit being such a bitch to everyone you meet, you'll find someone willing to put up with you." I gave her a forced smile. "I promise."

Her nostrils flared. "Of course. If I wanted it, which I don't, I could get my own little team of men."

She said this with such sarcasm, such disdain, it made me want to smack her face. She was looking down on me, when she'd done the exact same thing only years before. Except hers was based on a lie.

Power thrummed through my body. It rose up, a mighty dragon towering over her broken shell. It wanted to put her out again. Insubordinate, lying, scheming whore of a bitch. I took in a calming breath, trying to placate the power. I let out a strangled curse at her, forcing my will over my power. I was the master of my powers. Repeating

Christian's mantra, I shut it down, smothering it into a simmering flame.

Once I felt it was under control, I stood up, crossing my arms and faced her. I was done trying to help her feel better. "I have an assignment for you."

"You can't—"

"I can." I grit my teeth. "All assignments for the guys are on hold, give them to another team. They've been assigned something else, top priority."

"What? By whom?"

"None of your business."

She gave me a death glare.

"Just know that it involves the security of the Queen. As does your new assignment."

She opened her mouth, then shut it. "If it involves the security of the Queen, I'm at your disposal."

Even though I didn't trust her, Aria did. She held top secret clearance, so I could tell her the truth. "Your new assignment is to be put ahead of everything else. It's eyes only. If you fail, the Queen may die."

Her eyes focused on me; I had her attention now.

"For about two years, someone has been collecting items that weaken the Queen's power. Whoever has them is either destroying them or suppressing their power and that is affecting the Queen's magic." I paused, reminding myself again that Aria trusted her before I spoke the next words. "Her magic is tied to the Kingdom's artifacts."

Understanding dawned on her face. "The book."

I nodded. "That's why fixing the book was so important. We've hidden it, for now. But there are many other artifacts, and a lot of them have gone missing. She thinks that once whoever is stealing them will have enough, they're going to try to overthrow her. Or try to kill her." I paused to let the seriousness of my words sink in.

Sophia was fixing her ponytail again but I knew her mind wasn't on it. Her eyes were focused far away, thoughtful. She was trying to figure out who it was. Planning her next move.

"Sophia." She looked up at me. "They think that it's Andre."

She took in a sharp breath. "No. He would never."

"Your assignment is to determine if it's him, and what he's doing with the items. If he has any other plans. Can you do this?"

She didn't answer right away and I knew she was warring with her feelings. He came off as a cold, heartless bastard, but he'd taken her in. Did she harbor any love for him?

I continued. "Tell me the truth. If you can't, I understand. But this is too important for your pride to get in the way. Just be honest, and if you can't, we'll find someone else."

She looked into my face and nodded, cutting me off. Her eyes were clear, her face set. "Yes. I'll do it."

❦

CHRISTIAN AND EASTON CAME TO THE DOOR TO SEE SOPHIA OFF, WHO rushed off without much of a goodbye. I closed the door and turned to them. Now I had to deal with Avery.

"Christian."

"Yes?" As soon as he saw my determined face, he began to move back towards the living room. "I should probably finish the living room." It was already exactly the way it was before.

"Stop."

He halted, but still wouldn't look at me. Dark stubble marked his angular jaw line and he rubbed it thoughtfully. He looked sexy as hell.

"Do you know what happened with Avery?"

He suddenly turned away to inspect the frames on the wall. They were back in place but he straightened one that didn't need it.

"Christian!" He looked up at me and I punched his shoulder lightly, grinning. He was charming when he was avoiding me, even if he didn't mean to be. "Tell me."

He shrugged. "Maybe."

"Maybe my ass. Just tell me if you know."

Abruptly, he turned, pulling me to him and traced his finger down my cheek. Heat jolted in between my thighs and I leaned into him.

"I might know something." His green eyes pierced mine and I real-

25

ized that they looked different. His hold on my hip was possessive, his look on me, dominating. He was staking a claim, his claim on me. He ran his fingers down my neck and traced my collarbone. "What would this information be worth?" He raised his eyebrows and it made me shiver.

"Depends on what you're offering."

My comment was meant to be light but it landed with a dull thud in my chest. He wanted me all to himself. That's what he was offering and what I wasn't willing to take. I suddenly felt awkward.

He swallowed hard. "I will say one thing. Just know that Avery is very good at his job." He looked at me, expecting me to react.

Easton stepped in, saving me. "I wonder if Hunter's getting anywhere with him. If anyone could do it, it'd be him."

All three of us turned towards Avery's room at the same time.

I really wanted to know what they were talking about. "You guys thinking what I'm thinking?"

Both of them made a scramble for Avery's room at the same time. I thought for sure they'd break something else but they managed to jump over the couch and rush down the hall silently, despite their race to get there first. And now that my wolf powers were totally in check, I could run as fast and as silent as them.

I got there first, even though they had a head start. I smirked at them, they were half a second behind me. Oh yeah, wolf-Lizzy was a badass.

Christian grinned, coming in right behind me. He leaned against the wall and yanked me towards him. I fell into him and he turned me around so that my back was against his chest. Tucking me close, his fingers slipped under my shirt. Warm and spikey feelings raced through my body as he traced my stomach.

Christian was definitely staking his claim and it made my heart pound. I liked assertive Christian.

Easton stood next to me, leaning his head against the wall. He touched his foot against mine and I grabbed his hand, lacing my fingers through his.

Hunter was speaking. "Look, why don't you just tell us what happened. It could help."

"I'm going to pretend you didn't say that."

"But we're your team, we're allowed to know these things."

"Not this one. You know how it is, sometimes things can't be shared, even with the team."

Hunter's footsteps paced across the floor. "But Elizabeth is your Alpha now, you can at least tell her."

Avery didn't answer.

"I'm sure she can figure this out with you. She's growing closer to the Queen, maybe the Queen could do somet—"

"I just can't, okay?" Avery's voice grew louder, growing more frustrated.

"Why not?" Now Hunter was getting pissed.

There was a pause and the room was so silent, I couldn't even hear them breathe. Hunter's voice came out low, a deep growl.

"Avery."

Avery burst out, his voice desperate. "Because I screwed up, okay. I fucked up in ways that you can't even imagine."

Hunter didn't answer right away. When he did, his voice held a trace of vulnerability. "I know what screwing up on a job can do to you. To your family. I'll never forgive myself for what happened to my parents because of me." A sadness washed over me. Hunter's parents had been killed because of a screw up on one of his missions and he had to live with that for the rest of his life. "But hiding from it won't help."

"I'm not trying to hide from it. I'm trying to fix it."

"By leaving? That's not going to work. We need you on the team. Besides," Hunter's voice was firm, "I have a feeling that you need us. The only way to fix this is by doing it together."

"That's a lie." I heard Avery get off his bed and his drawers slide open. "Just let me go, okay? Maybe I'll come back. Once I fix this, maybe I'll see you and... and Lizzy again. But I need to fix this first."

Hunter growled. "Why don't you just tell—"

Avery burst out, interrupting him. "Because I can't look at her."

I took in a silent gasp, my stomach rolled with his words. Christian's fingers moved over my stomach in a soothing motion.

"What?"

"I can't look Elizabeth in the eyes and live with what I did. I just can't. It's killing me just seeing her. Just being around her. I can't breathe. I can't think. All I can do is just feel so fucking much for her that I would rather die than be around her right now."

My air was cut off as my heart squeezed in my chest. I wanted to burst in the room, to force Avery to talk to me. His words cut through me. What had he done? Why couldn't he just tell me?

Hunter's voice was low. "What the hell did you do?"

Avery's answer was just as low, and now it was threatening. "Hunter, get out of my way."

"No. If you can't tell her, then you will tell me. And you will tell me right now."

"Hunter, I have to fix this. And if you don't get out of my way, then I'll ma—"

"Stop!" Pulling out of Christian's embrace, I burst through the door. I couldn't take it anymore, and I couldn't let them say something they couldn't take back. "Just stop."

Christian and Easton entered with me, each of them looking like they were ready to jump on Avery. I took in a deep breath and it wheezed through my chest. Shit, it hurt so bad, the emotions filling me from everyone was too much. I leaned over, trying to stop the pain, to breathe. I gritted my teeth. "Would everyone just calm the fuck down?"

Hunter began to move towards me but I held out my hand. This wasn't about me. I took in a slow breath and stood up, putting my hands on my hips. "I need to speak to Avery. Alone."

Pushing down on his temper, Easton turned around and walked out of the door. "Just holler if you need help tying him down, I probably have some rope in my room." The sides of his lips twisted up in a mischievous grin. I had a feeling he did have rope in his room and that I was going to see it one day. I shivered, but turned to Christian. He gave Avery a meaningful look, then he caressed my cheek and walked out the door. I turned to Hunter, who didn't budge.

I looked into Hunter's eyes, pleading. "Please."

He hesitated, looking rebellious for a moment, then nodded his head. He brushed his fingers over mine as he left the room, and then it was just me and Avery, alone.

*a*very sat on his bed, not looking at me. I studied the pattern on his bedspread, noticing the way the different shade of blues and greys mixed together. Basically being distracted while I figured out how to start.

"You shouldn't listen at doorways."

I looked at him, his face was weary, his eyes clouded.

I sat next to him. "And you shouldn't come home, acting like an ass to the people who love you."

He jerked towards me, a scowl on his face. His beard made him look so damn sexy and rough and I wanted to run my fingers through it.

He didn't respond to my words, he just stared at me with his tortured eyes and it was breaking me in two. I needed to touch him. To feel his thrumming heart under my hands, the way I'd felt it that day by the waterfall. To hear the soft timbre of his voice move over my skin like silk. To see his burnt sienna-colored eyes look at me like he wanted me again.

"Lizzy." He took in a shaky breath and, fingers trembling, he touched my cheek. His eyes, so dark and cloudy, were intent on mine. "You can't fall for me. I can't be yours."

I inhaled a sharp breath. His words, so hard, cutting into me like broken glass, were opposite of his fingers that were caressing my skin. They were moving down my throat now and pulling down the side of my dress to bare my shoulder. I couldn't move, couldn't speak. I couldn't break the trance between us.

His fingers traced my shoulder lightly and then they moved down my arm, causing goosebumps as his fingers lightly traced the length of it. When he reached my fingers, he gripped them tightly, almost as if he were afraid of letting go. His other hand moved towards my chin and I held my breath in anticipation. He leaned forward, his eyes on my lips and suddenly I knew that he wasn't going to kiss me. He was going to kiss me goodbye.

I stood up, forcing his fingers to let mine go.

I knew that he wouldn't speak to me, tell me what was wrong. It was too early, he needed to process whatever he was going through. But I had to keep him with us long enough for him to do it. He needed a reason, besides me, besides the guys, to stay. Something he was more loyal to: his honor. So I took in a deep breath and for the second time in an hour, couldn't believe what I was about to say.

"Avery, you have a new assignment."

"What?" He stood up, facing me. "I can't. I would never tell you no under normal circumstances but there's something urgent I need to do."

I held out my palm, stopping him. "You're right. These aren't normal circumstances. Your new assignment is to protect the Queen. Unless whatever else you have going on has to do with an immediate need to save her life, this takes priority over everything else."

He stared at me with raging eyes, a stormy look on his face. But I ignored it and glanced at his clock, doing quick math.

"You have twelve and a half hours to get your shit together. Be ready tonight, at one-thirty a.m. sharp."

He opened his mouth to answer but I didn't let him. I was a freaking coward. I didn't want to hear him tell me no. Or whatever moody response he'd thought of. I turned around and jerked open the door. Christian and Easton jumped back in surprise, then fell over each other trying to scramble back, laughing.

"What the hell, guys?" I tried to give them a hard stare but a grin broke out at the guilty looks on their faces. I had no room to talk.

Christian stepped forward, pulling me out of Avery's room and into the hallway. His eyes stared into mine intently, but his face held a look of pride. "Good thinking." His words were soft, for my ears only. Then he spoke louder. "We need to plan what we're going to do."

Ignoring us, Easton took a step into Avery's room. "Get it together, man. We need you." He gave Avery a warning look, then grabbed the doorknob and slammed the door shut. Noises exploded behind it and I imagined Avery was throwing stuff around. Soon, loud, angry music filled the air.

I pushed away the desire to rush back into Avery's room and kiss all his pain away and allowed myself to be pulled by Christian and pushed by Easton down the hall.

๖ๅ

AFTER GRABBING MY BAG FROM ARIA, WE FOLLOWED THE SOUNDS OF Hunter into the kitchen. He was sitting at the table eating an apple. He smiled at me when I walked in but Christian's hand on mine tightened. He pulled me away from Hunter and led me towards the fridge.

It was obvious by the look on Hunter's face that he'd taken note of Christian's reaction. Instead of saying anything, he glanced towards the living room, and by extension, Avery's room. "That was fast. Did you tie him down?"

Christian and Easton smirked, but I shrugged. "Nope. Not yet, anyways." I paused, smiling. "I just basically told him to get over it. The Queen requested the team to work on a special project. It'll keep Avery busy for a little while. Hopefully long enough for us to figure out how to help him."

"Good idea." Grunting, Hunter leaned over the table and stared at the dark wood, still crunching on his apple.

Christian opened the fridge and began pulling out sliced ham, turkey, several avocados, mayonnaise, mustard and spinach. He handed the food to me and I placed them on the counter. Easton grabbed a loaf of sourdough bread from the pantry and pulled knives out of the drawer: one for cutting the avocado, and another for spreading the mayonnaise.

Letting Easton make the sandwiches, I grabbed the Queen's bag and began pulling everything out. I placed them neatly on the kitchen table, trying to ignore the tension building between Christian and the rest of the guys.

Tonight we were going to complete the first mission and we needed to focus.

Christian leaned over my shoulder, pulling me into him possessively and I glanced at the others. Easton threw me a smile, then kept making sandwiches. Hunter ignored us by examining the stuff on the table.

"What's this?" Christian pointed to a black case.

I opened it to show everyone. "It's the replica. We need to replace the original with this one."

"Oh, I know where that is. It's in the," Christian thought for a moment then snapped his fingers, "the Royal Institution of Legacies."

"Yep." I picked up the map of the inside of the museum and held it up so he could see it. I ran my finger over it, finding the location of the artifact. "That's where it's at. We need to go there, figure out what's the best entrance and the quickest route in and out."

He took it from me to study it and I noticed that Hunter was watching Christian's fingers on my hips. Easton handed me a sandwich.

"Thanks," I smiled at him. "So how does this work? How do you work together?"

Christian answered me. "Hunter is usually in charge of the mission, although technically you're in charge now. Usually Avery watches our back and handles the most dangerous weapons. Easton is in charge of anything electronic. Hunter is the planner and the manpower. He assesses the situation as we work, and makes any decisions while in the field. I'm in charge of handling civilians, if there are any, and dealing with unwilling captors. Of course, we can all do anything needed, and easily adapt if the situation calls for it."

I bit into my sandwich, thinking. Grabbing a napkin, Hunter wiped his fingers, then he stood up and put it and the core of his apple in the trash. When I finished chewing, I spoke my doubts. "I don't know if Avery is in the right space right now. I want him with us when we make the switch."

They all nodded their agreement and Hunter spoke up. "Do you know how to get inside?"

I nodded. "Yep. She gave me the codes. They change at midnight, every night. Usually the museums don't need that much security, but because of the artifact, security is tighter." I pointed to the paper in front of me. "These are the codes for after they change tonight. They'll gain us entry inside, to the alarm on the whole building, plus the individual ones that cover the artifact."

Hunter took the paper, studying it. "Since we already have the codes, Easton can do back-up instead of Avery." He looked up at Christian. "You think you can handle the alarm? Even if the codes don't work?"

Christian snatched the paper away. "Of course."

Hunter rolled his eyes and turned away from us to help Easton make more sandwiches. I squirmed in Christian's arms, feeling uncomfortable. Christian wasn't usually like this; he was usually the calmest one of the group. Something was making him act out. And, of course, I knew what that was.

I put my half-eaten sandwich on the table and turned in Christian's arms. I felt a little subconscious about what I was going to do, but I knew that I needed to do this, right in front of everyone. I grabbed Christian's face and, tugging softly on the back of his neck, I brushed my lips against his.

He froze, staring at me intently. The kitchen was silent and a soft blush marked my face, but I focused on him. He needed to know that he wasn't the last man I wanted and that I loved the way he touched me, the way he cared for everyone, the way he made me feel. That I wouldn't leave him behind, ever.

I put my hands to his face, cupping his cheeks, and the bond between us crushed me. Easton and Hunter were hard, like boulders demanding space in my life. Avery was the wind, blowing in and out of my life like a gale. But Christian, he was like water, softly filling in the spaces where the others lacked. A fire rose in my chest as a feeling of possessiveness overtook me.

I wouldn't let him go. I needed him in my life.

I stared into his eyes. "You are mine." I pulled him to me and claimed him with my lips. His breath caught in his throat, then he was responding with a rush of warmth against me. The world around me disappeared and it was him and me. His strong arms wrapped around me, pulling me tight, and I ran my hands through his hair, tugging on the back of his neck gently as my lips explored his. His tongue traced the edges of mine and I sucked it in deeper, running my tongue around it. He stiffened under me, his shaft growing stiff and I knew that he was a man who liked getting his dick sucked. Smirking to myself, I pulled his tongue in and out of my mouth, making him a promise. Letting him know that this was what I wanted and that he was going to get everything he ever wanted, and more. He grabbed the back of my head, pushing me in deeper as his lips explored mine.

Christian, soft and strong, protective and healing, a contradiction of existence. And mine.

After a while, I pulled back and he nibbled on the edge of my lips, tasting me one more time. His thumb rubbed my bottom lip and he stared into my eyes, a look of absolute possession on his face. "You belong to me."

I nodded. "Yes."

Suddenly, the tension in the room lowered, and Hunter sat back down, eating his sandwich and smirking at us. Christian took in a deep breath and looked around. Easton was eating and putting the food away at the same time.

Christian growled, letting out his sexual aggression. "Did you make me one?"

"Of course." Easton grabbed a paper towel and wrapped up the extra sandwich, then handed it over. Christian took it, then he let me go to help Easton put away the food. I grabbed the knives and washed and put them away, still holding my breath.

When they were done, Christian looked over at Hunter. "You ready to go?"

Hunter frowned, his mouth full. "Right now?"

Christian grinned. "Of course, man. When else?"

Hunter held up his finger, inhaling his food. "Give me a sec."

Easton pulled a set of keys out of his pocket and looked at Christian. "Let's go pack up the car. Hunter can drive, and we can finish our sandwiches in the car."

I picked up my half-way done sandwich. "Give me a sec with Hunter, guys."

Hunter grinned, looking up at me and I went to him, putting my sandwich on the table and sitting in his lap.

Christian bent over, kissing me softly and a warmth spread through my chest. I smiled and he winked at me, then left the kitchen, calling over his shoulder. "Come on, Eastie."

Grumbling at Christian's use of his new nickname, Easton cupped my face with both hands. His kiss wasn't soft, but demanding and all consuming. My face flushed with heat and I leaned up towards him, then he pulled away and looked at Hunter, who was casually leaning against the chair, still eating.

Hunter just raised his eyebrow. "You done?"

Grinning now, Easton strut out of the kitchen. "Yep."

ꙮ

I turned to look at Hunter. He smiled and brushed his bangs out of his face. I pulled my legs up, curling into his lap. I took in a deep breath and with it, his smell, and my tension began to melt away. I relaxed, feeling a lot better about the situation. I could make this work.

Putting his crust on the table, he wiped his hands on his jeans, then put his arms around me and I snuggled into his chest. We sat in silence for a while, each thinking our own thoughts. His fingers caressed my arms and it sent a wave of goosebumps down them.

I turned towards him, pulling my dress up so that I could straddle him. His fingers ran up my thighs and I bent down to softly brush my lips over his.

"I missed you, Hunter."

"Hmm." His voice was deep and soft, and it rumbled in his chest. "You have no idea how much I missed you."

"Don't ever get sick again."

He nodded, then he leaned down and, pulling my hand to his mouth, he raked his teeth across my knuckles, sending a shot of warmth down my body. His eyes stared intently into mine, his face was serious.

"Don't let me go. I need you, Elizabeth." He paused, his eyes searching mine. "I know you want us all. And I don't care. I will never leave you. I want to share you with the team."

His words washed over me, releasing me from the tension I'd felt inside, the stress of having to choose. I realized in that moment that I had been afraid. That even though they'd said I didn't have to choose only one of them, a small part of me feared that I would. That once I'd opened up, once I'd told them the truth -- that I couldn't choose -- their desire to keep me to themselves would come crashing down on me like a hurricane and I would loose them all.

But knowing that he was mine, that he would stay with me even though I couldn't let a single one of them go, pulled a thread of hope out of my heart that I hadn't dared pull.

"I fucking love you, Hunter." The words slipped out unbidden, unaware and unplanned, and my hand flew to my mouth. But they were the only words I could say, the only things I could think of to show my gratitude for the hope he was giving me.

He stared at me, his face open and filled with awe as silence filled the kitchen.

I cupped his cheeks, owning the words. "I do. I love you so much. I will never leave you. I choose you, too." And I meant it. I was choosing him. I was choosing them all but right here, right now, I was telling him that I wanted to be with him. I needed to say it, to let him know that I did love him. That I wasn't letting him go.

Emotion filled his eyes and then he was kissing my face. "I love everything about you. Your cheeks, your nose, your mouth." His lips moved over my cheeks, my nose, then he planted his mouth over mine in a deep kiss. I moaned, loving his fingers that were digging into my skin. His lips left mine and they moved to my neck, pressing soft kisses in the flesh.

"I love the way you talk and the sexy way you move when you sleep. I love the way you sigh and the way that you laugh, and even the way that you cry."

He pulled away to look into my eyes.

"I love the way that you look at me when you think I don't notice. You captivate me with your every move. I watch you, Lizzy, I can't help it." He gave me a serious look. "That's why I know you love me, because you say it in every thing that you do. And that is how I know that you love us all. You won't give up on Avery, just like you will also be able to give Christian what he needs to accept this. You give us everything that we need." His fingers tugged me close and he gave me another kiss, soft and tender. "That is one reason why I love you, Princess. Because you are everything we ever need. You fulfill us all."

I sucked in a breath, and the weight of the responsibility of making them all happy settled on my shoulders. It was a considerable burden. But the sincerity of his words, the honesty he showed me, gave me hope that I could do it. And, that they would all accept it, including Christian. That I could have my cake and fucking eat it to, smearing it all over my body and letting them lick it off me in one surge of selfish desire. That I could make each and every one of them happy, today and years from today. My necklace warmed at my chest, reminding me that I wasn't just some random wolf. I was born to be a leader, fated by the moon. I looked into his eyes and let my lips rest over his, giving him a gentle kiss.

"Thank you, Hunter."

Then Easton's voice called from the living room. "Come on guys, we don't have all day."

Hunter smiled. "Always the cock block, that one."

I grinned. "I'm sure you'll find a way to get him back one day."

He raised his eyebrow, grinning and thinking. "I'm sure there'll be plenty of opportunities."

WE SPENT THE REST OF THE AFTERNOON GETTING READY FOR OUR mission. We staked out the location, first with the satellite version of the GPS on their phone. Then we split up to do the rest of the recon on foot. Easton and Hunter walked the outside, casually noting any video cameras and all outside doors. They were also looking for a structure to set up in. So they walked the streets to determine how we would approach the building at night and all escape routes, if we ran into any problems.

Christian and I went inside and walked every inch of the museum. It was fairly open and I tried not to gawk at the art too much. There was so much beauty to see, and there was a special exhibit on dragons that probably couldn't be matched outside of the country. We noted each guard station and what surrounded the doors on the inside.

Christian walked with ease, his body relaxed, but his eyes were alert, taking everything in. My stomach was queasy. This would be my first official mission.

"We got this, Pinky. Don't worry. This will probably be one of the easiest missions I've ever had." Christian took my hand and stroked it softly. His healing power flowed through his hand, calming me and spiking my hormones all at once.

I loved that he knew when I needed his comfort. I loved that he was always watching out for me and the rest of the team. The simple act of his hand in mine set my hormones on fire and I clung to it, wishing we could be alone, wishing I could break through his walls, and wishing I could give him now what I'd promised him earlier.

My promise to have my lips on his bulging cock.

We kept walking and I checked him out of the corner of my eye. If I looked closely, I could see his dragon power pulsing from his body. It was strong and energetic, but it flowed through his body quietly. At peace with itself and with him. He had a strong connection to it.

He caught me staring and he flashed me a grin, showing his dimple. It made me smolder with need and his eyes darkened. We saw a door marked for employees only and Christian made a beeline for it. After checking to make sure it wasn't used often, Christian pulled me through it. As soon as we were on the other side of the door, he backed into the wall, pulling me to his chest. We were in an empty hallway, with a couple of closed doors on each side.

"Pinky." Christian's voice was a whisper, barely heard, and his finger went to his lips, telling me not to make a sound. We were wearing comms, in case we needed to communicate back and forth.

He pulled my chin forward and softly brushed his lips over mine. Electricity shot through my body and I wrapped my arms around his neck, pulling him close to press my lips against his. He grabbed my waist, tugging me in between his legs and then his tongue was tracing mine in a passionate kiss.

My breath was ragged as every sense lit on fire and with Christian's legs squeezing me between them, he was making it impossible for me to think. All I could imagine was his legs surrounding me, riding me like a fucking warrior. His hands tangled in my hair, tugging the ends softly, then they traced softly down my back. They broke through the bottom of my shirt and lightly caressed my skin.

I arched my back, pressing against his chest, still kissing him and rubbing myself against him. My hands cupped his face, pulling him to me, loving his touch, loving his fingers on my skin, his lips on mine, his tongue in my mouth. My whole body was on fire, wanting, needing.

I needed more of him, not these tidbits he was feeding me.

I released our kiss and fell to my knees, running my hands down his chest as I fell. Then I put my hands to his snap and looked up at him, showing him what I wanted to do.

"Lizzy." His whispered voice was mixed with a warning and desire.

I pulled the comm out of my ear and threw it to the side. He hesitated, just for a moment then, glancing down the hallway, he took his out and tossed it away gently. Grinning, and about to burst with need, I popped the snap to his jeans and slowly pulled down his zipper. I reveled in the sound, loving the darkness in his eyes as he watched me, loving the way the zipper snapped when I pulled it all the way down.

His breath came in and out as I reached in, and then his skin on my fingers was like lightning, shooting up my body. He leaned his head back against the wall as I pulled his dick, aching with want, out. It was nestled in thick wiry blonde hair, straining, proud and hard, up to his stomach.

I stared at it, honoring it, worshipping it and I bent forward, unable to stop myself from licking the pre-come leaking out of the top.

He let out a guttural moan and I closed my mouth over the tip, needing to taste him.

Shit.

He tasted salty and spicy and bitter all at once and it was a raging rock just for me. It lit my lips on fire and I couldn't get enough. The skin was silky smooth and I explored it, swirling my tongue over the swollen tip. His hands gripped the top of my head, urging me lower and I couldn't stop my own moan now; it was turning me on to see how hard he was for me.

I moved up and down, sucking hard, taking him all the way in to the back of my throat. His hands on my hair were egging me on and my own emotions were spiking. I was afraid I was going to come, just from the thought of him in my mouth. His need pressing into my own.

Fuck, it was such a turn on.

I moved one of my hands to lightly massage his sac and he bucked his hips, aching with so much need.

I wanted to fulfill it. To be his fix. To give him everything he ever needed or wanted. To swallow his cum, so that he and I were together, at last.

The concrete floor at my knees bit into my skin harshly and the air on my back made me shiver. The fact that we were in a hallway where anyone could walk in and see us only made my panties wet. I wanted to show the world how I felt about him.

But I quickened my pace so we wouldn't tempt fate, bobbing my head up and down. He was moving with me, thrusting inside me, and I could tell by the look on his face that he was going to come soon. I gripped the bottom, squeezing it tight and moaned, sending vibrations up through his shaft.

He came into my mouth and I took it all in, licking and squeezing until I licked every drop.

"Fuck, Pinky," he whispered. "That was so fucking hot."

He was breathing heavy and I licked and softly scraped my teeth against his hips. Then I stood up, pushing up his shirt to softly bite and lick his chest up to his neck. I nuzzled my chin in the crook of his neck while zipping his jeans. "That's only the beginning. I'm going to give you everything you want, any time you want it. You just have to say the word, and I'm yours."

He nodded, wrapping his arms around me, holding me for a moment. He felt looser, more relaxed and I grinned, realizing that this is what he needed. Then he turned his face to softly bite my shoulder. "You're next."

4

*E*verything was all planned, down to the smallest detail and I only had one thing left to accomplish. My eyebrow raised as I stared at the slick black uniform. We were back at the house and everyone, including a serious and straight-faced Avery, was getting ready to go.

I checked the tags again. Yep, it was my size. But it looked a hell of a lot smaller. Steeling myself, I stretched, tugged, and yanked the black uniform until finally, the pants and shirt were attached to my body. It didn't feel like I was wearing the uniform, more like it was wearing me.

Manly voices rumbled down the hallway and I knew that they were ready. I rushed forward, grabbing my socks and boots. I fell back onto my bed, bending over to pull them on and my uniform moved instantly, clinging and molding to my skin. I stood up, smiling, and jumped and swirled in the air, testing it. I had no freaking clue what material the uniform was made out of, but it was soft, silky, and moved and stretched with every motion.

By the time I walked out of my room, they were all waiting for me at the front foyer. I literally gasped when I saw them, all standing there in a row.

Wrapped in tight, black shirts and loose cargo pants, with laced up combat boots, they looked like mercenaries from hell. Except sexy ones. Sexy hellions. Their expressions darkened as they took me in and their chatter stuttered to a stop. Each one of them stared at me, their eyes traveling up my body and I suddenly felt very self-conscious.

"What?" I noticed that they all had guns tucked into holsters at their hips. "Hey! Where's my gun?"

Hunter chuckled but Easton's eyes just burned into me. Stepping forward, Christian pulled on my belt loop, dragging me to him. "You get a gun when you complete your certification."

I folded my arms across my chest. "I know how to use one."

He nodded. "Oh, I know. I remember a very steady hand on the gun you pointed at me."

I furrowed my brows. "I didn—"

He gripped my chin, pulling my face to his. "Oh, yes you did. You haven't forgotten how we met, have you?" His lips were so close to mine and I remembered what we'd done in the hallway. It made my lips burn at just the thought of it.

And then, the memory of the first time I saw Christian came to my mind. Me, pointing my gun towards him and saying, "Don't come a step any closer." And then I'd cocked the gun. I cocked it.

I blushed. "Whoops!"

He stared into my eyes and focused on my face. "It was actually pretty damn hot."

There was a movement behind me. Avery. He gripped the gun holstered to his hip and looked away. Easton was still staring a hole into me, but Hunter was shoving something into a bag.

I looked back at Christian, ignoring the heat that was flushing up my face. "You looked pretty damn hot yourself." I leaned into him, tracing his lips with my finger. He nipped at them, then smiling, he kissed me full on the mouth.

I hugged him close, gripping my hands around his waist. When he pulled back, I grabbed Easton and tugged him into our embrace and kissed him. Smirking, Easton's lips moved over mine and his hand wrapped around my waist and then down to squeeze my ass. I grinned and let him go.

Avery was still looking away but Hunter stepped towards me. "I've got your bag." He held it up. He also had another one over his back.

"Thanks." I smiled and he gave me a light brush over my lips, then he walked out the door with a command that everyone head out. I walked up to Avery and pulled softly on his beard. He turned to look at me, his face tight but his eyes, deep and probing, stared right into my soul.

"I like your beard."

He swallowed hard. "I know."

"That's why he hasn't shaved it yet." Christian gave me a knowing look and disappeared out the front door. Easton grabbed his bag, slung it over his back and left, leaving Avery and I alone.

"Is that true?" I looked at Avery.

He nodded.

"How did you know?"

The side of his lips lifted and he stepped forward, putting his head on mine. "I just know you, Lizzy."

Warmth washed over me. Lizzy.

Cautiously, I palmed his face in my hand. When he didn't push me away, I ran my hands through his beard. It was so rough on my hand and so fucking sexy. I wanted to feel it prickle against my face. I reached up, my eyes on his lips. His hand went to my hip, digging his thumb into it. He was pulling me closer with his fingers but pushing me away with the palm of his hand. It made him press into my side, stilling me.

"Lizzy." His voice was a warning.

Wrapping my hand around the back of his neck, I tugged him closer. I leaned my cheek against his, rubbing it against his beard, and a wave of heat rushed through me. Damn, it felt so good. Avery felt so good against me.

Giving in to his warring feelings, his firm, lean body pressed into me.

My breath caught. I swallowed the lump in my throat, making a decision. Making the decision that Avery was fucking mine, and I wouldn't let him go. There would be no transferring to another team, no running away.

I trailed my hand down his chest slowly, still rubbing my cheek against him. He held his breath as my hand moved slowly down his stomach to the top of his pants. His eyes were closed but I knew that he could sense every movement, every touch. I pressed my chest into him, still rubbing his cheek with mine.

I was going to make him see it, make him want me. And I was going to Make. Him. Beg.

I cupped him, feeling his raging erection which was pressed tight against his zipper. I rubbed my finger over the top of his pants, briefly brushing across his tip and a deep rumble came from his chest. His breathing came in and out in shallow flutters and I hooked my finger at the top of his pants, playing with the snap. All it would take was one pull, one tug, and his dick would be in my hands. I paused, drawing out the tension as I moved my lips closer to his.

Then I pulled away, turned around and walked out the door. "Don't want to keep them waiting."

⚚

TRYING NOT TO LAUGH LIKE THE CRUELLA DE VIL, I SCOOTED INTO THE back seat of the black Range Rover SUV, a grin on my face. It smelled like leather and the musky scent of masculinity. It seeped into my skin, reminding me of my time with them at the cabin back in Tennessee. For a brief moment, sadness clung to me, reminding me of home.

Hunter was driving with Easton in the passenger seat, and Christian held his hand towards me from his spot in the back. I grabbed it and he pulled me next to him on the backseat bench.

All eyes were on me, hungry and needy, and I shivered. I must look

46

hella good in this uniform. I mentally strutted and settled in next to Christian's muscular body.

All at once, all eyes shifted to the house and I turned to see Avery slam the front door. By the looks of his pants, he'd taken a second to wrangle his hormones under control. He slid into the back seat beside me, giving me a deathly glare. "Where are we going and what am I doing?" He sounded very angry.

He also hadn't participated in the planning, so he had no idea what we were doing.

Hunter's eyes watched Avery in the rearview mirror, waiting for him to shut the door. Easton was also staring at Avery but both him and Christian were grinning like the cat that just ate the canary. They all knew that something had happened in the house, but I just smirked, saying nothing.

"What the hell am I doing?" Avery repeated himself, his voice even lower and more gruff. When no one answered him right away, he slammed his door shut, then folded his arms across his chest, staring out the window.

Even though there was plenty of room for each of us on the seat, both Christian and Avery pressed into my side. Christian put his hand on my thigh and leaned in close to whisper in my ear. "What did you do to him in there?"

"I can hear you." Avery didn't look towards us but kept staring out the window.

Christian leaned even closer and the smell of salt and wind assaulted my senses, sending them into overdrive and his hand edged higher up my thigh, caressing me softly with his thumb. He whispered louder this time. "He looks like he needs a good screw. And he wishes that screw was you."

Suddenly Avery was around me, slamming his fist into Christian's chest. The guys burst out into laughter and Avery turned his fists onto Easton's shoulder. When no one hit him back, he slumped back into his seat, still leaning against me. "Just tell me what I need to do, alright?"

&

WE DROVE INTO THE CITY AND HEADED STRAIGHT FOR THE CENTER. AS
Easton gave Avery instructions, Christian stroked my thigh with his
thumb and it was sending shooting waves of heat up my body. His
breath was on my neck every time he spoke, and that was shooting
shivers down my spine. His desire pressed into my senses, sparking my
own until a slow tinkling of jealousy from Avery began to leak into my
feelings. I was bombarded by emotions from both sides: Christian's
determination to take a step towards claiming me and Avery's angry,
jealous, and burning desire. He wanted me but he also wanted to leave.
He wanted to make things right but he also wanted to fly away and
never return. Even though his arms were folded across his chest with his
hands closed into fists, he still leaned against me, squeezing me in
between him and Christian. Every time we turned the corner, his elbows
brushed against the tips of my boobs, causing them to perk happily.

I was almost certain it was deliberate. He was getting me back for
what I did to him at the house. Every instinct in my body told me it
was on purpose but I wasn't exactly sure because his face was an
opaque mask of grumpy.

To make matters worse, adrenaline was coursing through my body
because I was going on my first mission ever and I had no idea what
the hell to expect. I knew what I was supposed to do, of course.
Hunter ran through it with me until I knew every detail, every act.
And yet, I still had this nagging feeling that we should expect the
unexpected. That we'd forgotten something. That something wasn't
right.

I was trying not to hyperventilate as we pulled up to the back alley.
As soon as Christian opened his door, I scrambled over him and
jumped out of the car and ran up the street.

I needed space from them for just a minute.

I was a block away before I even realized what I was doing. I froze,
feeling like an idiot and turned back around. They all just stared at me
with their damn hotness, their damn fucking mercenaries from hell

sexiness and it notched up my emotions. If we weren't about to do something majorly important, I would force them all back into the car and screw them all, one by one, until I passed out from too much sex. Was that possible?

Probably.

Maybe?

Forcing an easy smile, I jogged back towards them, trying not to look like I'd just bolted from my four sexy guys. Christian smirked at me and I scowled at him, which made him burst into a grin. Karma is a bitch.

Gah.

"You okay?" I felt Hunter's concern for me. He handed me an earpiece.

I smiled up at him. "Yep. No problems. I'm just fine." His look told me he didn't believe me but I didn't say anything else. I put the speaker thingee in my ear and Hunter clipped it to the front of my uniform, his fingers lingering over my collarbone.

"Hunter." Easton's face was serious. "Get your head in the game." He looked at Christian and Avery. "You too, guys. Let her focus."

Avery looked away, scowling, but Christian's smile only grew bigger. "Oh, my head's in the game, alright."

Hunter didn't respond to Easton, but handed me my bag while all the guys opened theirs and suddenly we were all business. We pulled out bulletproof vests and Hunter helped me strap into mine.

"Are we really going to need these?"

His look was firm. "We hope for the best and plan for the worst. We never take chances."

I swallowed, completely sobering up even though the vests increased their hotness by about a thousand percent. "Of course."

Easton sat in the back of the SUV and opened his laptop. We waited until he hacked into the cameras and replaced it using the video feed from Aria.

While we waited, I watched Easton's fingers on his laptop, his eyes scrunched at the screen with his glasses on. I decided to make him teach me that stuff one day. After a while, he looked up at me, smiling. "Done."

I tried to smile back at him, but I was too nervous. He shut his laptop and pulled on the hook, opening the floor of the SUV. He placed his computer in a special compartment, then shut the door. I heard the latch clamp in place. You'd need the code to open it again.

Ready now, Hunter looked at Christian. "Christian, you take point. Then Elizabeth. Avery backs her up." Just like we'd planned.

Since I had no experience in missions, Hunter was in charge tonight.

Serious now, Christian stepped ahead and I followed behind him.

Our mission was to be invisible. To silently slip in and out of the museum, replacing the artifact and, hopefully, without a hitch. Our number one priority was to get the real artifact. Number two was to do it unnoticed.

Compared to most of the other ops my guys had participated in, this one was easy. The museum wasn't considered a high target for thieves, mostly because the artifacts' power being tied to the queen was super hush-hush. It also had a highly sophisticated alarm system, which would be no problem for us since we had the codes.

All of my guys were focused but relaxed and the only concern I felt from them was for me. My own tension was leaking into them, so they were worried about me.

We were silent now and I fell in line, smooshed between Christian and Avery. Literally. Avery was walking so close to me that I felt the need to walk faster. But Hunter told me to stay behind Christian, so I was right on his heels. He kept pausing every so often to make sure that I was behind him, and so most of the time either Avery or Christian were touching me.

Hunter was ahead of the whole group while Easton brought up the rear. This part of the city was clean and quiet, with only sleeping blocks of apartment homes and ornately designed businesses. There was no one on the street and very few guards expected inside.

I should feel relaxed. Being with experienced teams, who had done things a lot harder than this should've given me a lot of confidence.

Except that there was a nagging feeling at the back of my mind. The feeling that there was a small possibility that Andre would have somehow gotten word that we'd be coming in tonight. That and the fact that he probably wasn't too happy that Hunter and I had sex on his desk.

Yeah. There was that too.

So, a good reason for him to want to kill two birds with one stone. Get the artifact. Kill the annoying pests that soiled his desk.

Hunter splintered from the group, walking north while we continued west. After three blocks, Christian, Avery and I headed north while Easton disappeared through the door to a parking deck.

There were three entrances to the building. One in the front and one in the back, then an inconspicuous one on the side. The front entrance would be occupied by two guards and would have the most traffic, if any, at this time of night. The side door was next to an apartment building, which could have late-night stragglers, so we were entering through the back exit.

Easton was going to cover our back exit by setting up on the parking deck next to it. Hunter was going to watch the side exit. The front exit would go unwatched, since it was covered by the guards. We would use that door as an absolute last resort.

As soon as we reached the museum, we stopped in the shadows, watching the door from across the street. The back end of the museum was still beautiful; it looked like a small palace.

While we waited for clearance from Hunter and Easton, both guys pressed into my side and it was making me anxious. My restlessness was leaking into them, in turn making them nervous. I could feel it in every inch of my body and their touch was only making it worse.

"Do you guys always keep so close to each other on missions?" I whispered frantically, even though no one was on the streets.

"What's going on over there?" Easton's voice came out clearly through the earpiece. Both Avery and Christian jumped apart.

"Nothing." I held my hand to my ear like someone in the movies, even though it clearly wasn't necessary. "Nothing going on. You just let us know when we're clear to go in." I forced confidence that I didn't feel into my words.

Christian yanked his earpiece out and turned towards me. "Everything's going to be fine, Pink. Just calm down. Even if something happens, we've got each other's back." He stared into my eyes and I focused on his words. "Plus, we've got badass Lizzy on our team. This is a walk in the park." He winked, taking my hand in his and shot a calming warmth into it. I took in a deep breath, letting go of my nervousness. He was right. Even if Andre showed up, we could handle it.

"Better?" His green eyes focused on my response. I nodded and he smiled. Kissing the top of my head, he put his earpiece back in. Avery squeezed my hand reassuringly, and I smiled at him.

Then we were back in mission mode as Hunter's voice sounded in my ear. "All clear on my end. How you doing Eastie?"

I sniggered, amused that Easton's new nickname was catching on.

"You call me that again and you'll be eating my fist for breakfast."

"I'd like to see you try, Eastie-boy."

I cupped my hand over my mouth, grinning. Avery didn't look affected but Christian had a smile on his face.

"I've got no problem with that." Easton again. "I'm all clear on my end. I also checked your front door on my way here. Everything is a go."

Christian bounced off the wall and I followed him, with Avery on my tail. We kept to the shadows except to cross the dark street. A grey and orange cat emerged and raced in front of us, its tail held high. It was headed straight for the large trash bin behind a seafood restaurant. I knew it served seafood because I could smell the fishy rank from where I walked.

We reached the museum and stopped under a window. Christian waited a sec, then he peered inside. After making sure that no one was in the back room, Christian led us to the door. He punched in the code and the door opened. We had exactly ten-seconds to disable the silent alarm.

CHRISTIAN RUSHED FORWARD AND EASILY PUT IN A COMPLEX SERIES OF numbers. The blinking red light turned to green and he gave us a thumbs up.

"So far, the codes are good." Christian reported to Hunter and Easton. Avery pressed into me, pushing me gently forward and we fell in line again, walking through the hallways, passing glorious and beautiful pieces of art.

After passing several rooms, Christian stopped outside a doorway. In the next room was the guard station located in the middle of the museum. Information from Aria, plus Christian's and my surveillance, determined that there were only four guards on duty at night. Only one covered this station and he was busy watching the soccer game. Just as we'd anticipated. Tonight was the first game of the season and everyone and their dog were watching it. It was popular here in Aerwyna.

He looked at Avery, speaking softly. "Your turn."

He moved forward, and they switched positions with me still squished in the middle like the jelly in a peanut butter sandwich. The guys were the peanut butter, of course, because they had the nuts.

Avery pulled something out of his bag, then crouched to the ground, motioning for us to do the same. We silently slid down the wall, opening our backpacks, while Avery slithered on his stomach and disappeared around the corner, holding a canister of sleeping gas.

After a few seconds, Avery climbed back around the corner and we all put our gas masks on. With a slight hiss, gas leaked from the container throughout the alcove next to us. I counted silently in my head, waiting for it to knock the security dude out, and I could hear either Hunter or Easton breathing in my ear. I breathed loudly through my gas mask as the minutes ticked by.

"What the hell?" The security guard finally noticed the gas. His footsteps were slow and heavy as he moved closer to us. There was a loud thump and then the room was silent. After a beat, Avery peeked around the corner, then stood up and we moved towards the security guard who was now taking a nice nap on the floor. He was probably going to wake up with a hell of a headache.

"Spray this around. It'll disperse the gas and the smell." Avery's voice came to me through the earpiece as he handed me an aluminum canister. He and Christian picked up the guard and took him towards his chair. I grabbed the can off the floor and tucked it into my backpack, then sprayed the air, dispersing the gas.

Soon, the guard was propped back into his chair, like he'd just fallen asleep on the job. The monitors next to him showed an empty room, as planned.

As soon as it was clear, we tucked our masks away and moved quicker through the museum. As long as the two guards at the front entrance stayed up there, we would only have to watch out for one more. We went through a large room made of a long wall of windows and the light from the moon highlighted several old statues.

"There it is." Christian pointed to a mask sitting on a black stand. It was highlighted by a sharp light and covered by a glass casing. Christian left Avery and me to walk towards the back wall.

While we waited for him to disarm the alarm over the artifact, Avery pulled out the replica and I studied the original. It was a mask. It had a green face with yellow hair, sculpted by hands a thousand or two years ago. It was actually pretty ugly, but it looked old as sin and maybe they had different tastes back then. The hair stretched out from the head in wavy lines, almost like it had a mind of its own. The mouth to the mask was open and a snake with purple and green markings, slithered from its lips.

It was a representation of the creator from which the scaled snake crawled out of his mouth. From that snake came the first dragon.

Compared to the replica, the artifact had a more mysterious and beautiful quality to it. It pulsed a mesmerizing golden glow and I realized I was seeing the magic contained within it. I squinted at Avery, looking to see if he was as captivated with it as I was.

His face was serious; he stared at it more like it was a bomb.

"Do you think that dragons really came from a snake?"

Avery gave me a strange look. "You think powerful dragons came from a snake?"

"I don't know. That's why I'm asking you." I nodded towards the mask. "That's what this myth is about, anyways."

"That's just one myth. There are a ton of others."

"So which one is the truth?"

"Does it matter?" Avery's face was a scowl.

I shrugged. "Maybe it matters to me. I want to know where you guys come from. If I'm going to have your babies, I need to know what's going to be growing inside of me."

Noises exploded in my ear as Hunter and Easton reacted to my words.

"What the hell, woman?" Easton's voice growled in my ear. Hunter was only sucking air through his teeth and out of the corner of my eye, I could see Christian's hand frozen on the panel.

Avery's eyes were wide as he stared at me.

I touched my stomach. "That's what all this is about, isn't it? Having dragon babies." I was trying to get a reaction from him, just to wipe that scowl off his face. And I'd succeeded, because now he was staring at me like a snake was going to come out of *my* mouth. "The least you could do is give me the courtesy of telling me what your theories are."

His mouth opened and he gasped at me like a fish. I smirked, trying not to laugh, but then Christian's voice was in my ear. "It's disarmed."

Even though Avery's face was still a mask of shock, he didn't miss a beat. He handed me the replica and gingerly pulled off the glass. Then he gently took the antique mask off the stand and carefully placed it inside the case.

The case was slim enough to carry easily but large enough to protect the mask. It was padded and lined with a bulletproof casing. If it did its job right, it would protect the mask from almost anything.

I eyed it warily as he latched it shut. It better do its job, I wasn't sacrificing my guys anymore for the Kingdom. Then he strapped it to the front of his chest. He didn't want to leave it at his back, unprotected.

I gingerly placed the replica on the stand and Avery moved the glass case back over it. Pushing the locks in place, he spoke to Christian.

"Put the alarm back on."

Giving me a wary eye, Avery gripped my hand and we moved back in the same direction we came from. After a minute, I felt Christian's hand on my shoulder. "Ready."

They switched positions and we were back in our peanut butter and jelly sandwich.

We passed easily through the rooms and Christian reported on our progress to Hunter and Easton. We stopped only once to wait for the roaming guard to pass by, then proceeded towards the back offices of the museum. When we reached them, we paused and Christian spoke.

"Waiting for the all clear to leave the museum."

There was a pause and then Easton spoke. "Hold up." Suddenly, the nervousness I'd felt earlier was back and I waited anxiously. His voice came through the comms. "There's a procession of black vans headed towards my door."

Suddenly the easy going mood from my guys was replaced with a laser focus: complete the mission. Get everyone out safely.

5

"*S*hit." Hunter sounded pissed. Avery grabbed the back of my shirt and Christian instantly took two steps backwards; they were squeezing me between them.

"Ok," Hunter was in charge now. "Avery and Christian, start towards my door. I'm going to move to get a better view up my street. If you encounter anyone, use evasive measures as much as possible; the Queen can't be connected to us. If trouble comes, do not engage unless it's to save a life."

I tried not to freak out but it was hard to swallow down the fear pushing up my chest, choking off my air. My instincts had been spot on. We turned around and quickly, but steadily, made our way towards the side door. Avery didn't let my shirt go and his elbow pressed against my back, urging me forward. Christian grabbed his gun, flicked off the safety and held it tightly to his side.

Easton spoke again. "Three SUVs pulled up to the door and three more kept going. Hunter, I think they're headed your way."

"I'm on the lookout." Hunter.

Avery grabbed my hand and we began to sprint through the building with Christian in the lead. There was no way around it, the security guards were going to hear us. We raced straight through the rooms, weaving through the sculptures and art pieces. My wolf was on full alert, ready to shift if necessary. I held her back. If I shifted in front of the guards, they would know it was me.

Easton spoke again. "Five men have exited each vehicle. Fifteen men are now entering my side. They've brought weapons. It's a no-go on this exit. Hunter?"

"Shit. Confirming three vans are pulling up to my door. Avery and Christian, protect her with your life. Everyone meet at the front door, I'll bring the car. Easton, get to the front doors as fast as you can."

We raced around the corner and Christian collided with the security guard.

"Hey!" The guard landed in a heap. His paunch belly stuck out like a white beached whale. Christian grabbed him, yanking him to his feet, then began dragging him with us. Avery's hand tightened on mine, pulling us forward.

The guard tripped over his feet and caught himself on Christian. Then he tried to yank his hand out of Christian's grasp, but Christian's hand was a steel trap. Christian glanced at the guard. "Radio to your men at the front desk, tell them to get the hell out of here."

"Get your hands off me. I'll call in the police."

Christian suddenly stopped, pulling the man close. His eyes were serious as hell, his face a scowl. "If your men don't get out of here right now, they will die. Tell them to leave now."

The guard just stared at him, his mouth agape. "How, how—"

"Do it now!" Christian's voice came out a bark. The guard scrambled for the radio pinned to his shoulder, his eyes wide.

"We have a Code Yellow. This is not a drill."

"What—" A response squawked over the radio.

"This is not a fucking Code Yellow." Christian was dragging the guard again who scrambled to catch up. "Tell them it's a fucking Code Red."

Taking in Christian's uniform, the guard hit the button on his radio again. "Code Black. I repeat, this is a Code Black. Press the alarm and take your positions."

Suddenly, a change came over the guard. He jerked himself out of Christian's grasp and sprinted forward. He was fast. Faster than I thought possible for his large stature. We followed him, trusting that he knew the quickest route out.

Suddenly a loud boom roared through the museum.

❧

WE HESITATED IN SHOCK, JUST FOR A MOMENT, AND THEN WE WERE running again. Dragon magic pulsed through the room and I pushed it away with my own magic. Otherwise it would suffocate me.

The guard ran to a closet and pressed in four numbers on the keypad. Yanking it open, he grabbed a deadly looking weapon. We raced past him, headed towards the sound of utter chaos.

We stopped just before entering the front entrance, listening to the blasting sounds of guns.

"We're at the front." Christian glanced at me, making sure I was with them.

Easton's voice was in our ear again. "I'll be there in two."

Avery was still beside me, pulling out his gun. My heart hammered in my chest. I put my hand over my necklace. Its pulsing warmth was comforting. Two guards were stationed behind a large mahogany desk, each holding a rifle that was trained on the front. Large black disks shaped like turtle shells covered the front of the desk. Bullets were slamming into it, then ricocheting into the room. The guards peeked out every so often to take a shot.

Christian took in the room. "There are approximately seven men coming through the front door, with more coming in. Three are down by the three guards from the museum. Two museum guards have rifles and one has a dragon's breath."

"Copy." Hunter's voice. "I'm in the car, headed your way."

Suddenly, the guard charged around the corner, passing by us without so much as a glance. Christian watched him pass then looked at Avery. "Keep her safe. Our priority is getting out. If possible, saving the guards."

He didn't wait for Avery to respond but stepped out into the chaos. I took a breath, then followed him out. Adrenaline rushed through my body. Sweat poured down the front of my shirt. All my senses were heightened. My wolf panted, ready to burst out of me.

I could see now that the whole front door was blasted open. Soldiers were blocked from entering by the shooting from the guards. The first guard made it past the open space to the desk unhurt. He was setting up his weapon.

Another two booms reverberated through the room. That meant the other doors were down. We were going to have to fight our way out. And fast. Before reinforcements surrounded us.

Ducking low, we scrambled towards the desk. A bullet zoomed towards me and Avery pushed me forward. I shot forward towards the desk, landing with a slide next to a guard. Christian and Avery landed right behind me.

I stared up at Avery with wide eyes. He held out his hand and I grabbed it. He pulled me up.

"Thanks."

He just grunted.

Hunter was in our ear. "I'm about three minutes out. Easton, where are you?"

"I've just turned the corner. I can see about ten men out here. They have a tank set up. I'm taking out the ones I can."

"Shit." Hunter's voice was deep. He was definitely pissed now. "Who the hell sent the freaking army out?"

Christian spoke. "Easton, get back."

The first guard suddenly stood up like a motherfucking champion, facing the wall of men and bullets. He looked through a long scope and pressed the trigger. The room shook from the weapon's noise and a burst of light flew across the room. About twenty feet across, it erupted into a large ball of fire. It landed on the group of men who were too slow to get out of its way. It quickly spread across them in a blaze. I stared, open mouthed as bodies turned to ash.

Christian and Avery, along with the museum guards, took advantage of the distraction. They shot at any remaining guards. There was another boom as a tank barreled into the museum, taking out a section of the wall. The first guard took another shot with his fire-breathing weapon.

I held my breath as it landed on its target. Fire spread quickly but the tank rolled forward, undeterred. Bursts of light came from the tank, taking out the first guard next to me. He fell forward, the desk catching him, and his blood pooled on the desk.

Shit. We weren't going to make it against a freaking tank. Everyone was shooting at each other. My mind churned, trying to figure out how to get out of this.

Suddenly, I had a thought.

"Hunter, the museum has a wall of windows. Where the artifact was. Meet us there."

Easton answered me. "I know where that is. I have two more out here, then I'll meet you there."

Hunter answered. "On my way."

I could hear men converging on us from all sides. They were going to be here soon. I closed my eyes, focusing on my power. It pulsed and throbbed, flowing and ebbing through my body. "Guys, get ready to run towards that room."

Christian and Avery both nodded, then tugged on the other guards.

I stood up, with a sudden burst of energy I pushed my power towards the tank. A blue ball of energy slammed the tank, throwing it towards the back wall.

Suddenly, a group of soldiers rushed into the room from the other side. Avery grabbed the torchlight and shot towards them. They scrambled out of the way and we made our break.

We sped through the halls and fur erupted on the back of my neck and hands. A tingle moved over my whole body. My wolf felt the need to protect me. But I didn't want the guards to know who I was. Christian was leading the way, just one step ahead of Avery and me. Thank heavens Avery pushed me to run in Hawaii. I hadn't stopped since I came here so I wasn't out of breath as we sprinted through the rooms. The other two guards weren't that far behind us.

Suddenly shots boomed out and I heard one of the guards cry out. I didn't look back. I couldn't. I couldn't bear to see someone else die because of our mission. Christian glanced behind me then grabbed my hand and yanked me forward so that I was leading.

Everything around me disappeared from my vision. All the beautiful artwork that was probably being destroyed by flying bullets. The walls, the doorway. The only thing I focused on was the trinkle of moonlight I could see up ahead.

We burst into the room and headed towards the wall of windows. Another group of men poured in from the other side. We were completely surrounded.

The only way out was the wall of glass.

Suddenly a man appeared in the windows. He was different than the rest. He wasn't wearing the same uniform. He also wasn't holding on to a rifle. He raised his glock, aiming right for me.

Wings burst from Avery's back, pushing him in front of me. Christian tackled me from behind, shoving me towards the floor. I fell, skidding across the floor.

I turned towards Avery, he was leaning over. I screamed as fear slammed into my body. Instant rage poured over me. I scrambled to my feet, furious, and ran towards the man. A window panel was shot out. He swiveled his gun, aiming for me again.

I shot my blue magic towards him. Glass erupted, cascading to the floor with a tinkling roar as my magic broke through it. It slammed into his body, throwing him back. At the perfect moment, the Range Rover sped into view and slammed into him, propelling him across the street.

He landed with a thud, and blood drained from his mouth. Easton ran up, his eyes on the man on the ground.

I turned around and Christian was hauling Avery towards the car. The last guard lay on the ground, dead.

Hunter rolled down the window. "Get in the car!"

His words woke me, and I ran through the broken windows. I jumped into the street, passing Avery and Christian. I opened their door. Christian threw Avery inside, and then he grabbed my vest and shoved me in. Easton climbed in the passenger seat; he looked ready to punch someone. Hunter shot forward and down the street while Christian scrambled inside and slammed the door shut. Bullets pinged off our car as we sped down the street.

⚜

MY SENSES IMMEDIATELY TUNED TO EVERY SOUND IN THE CAR, listening for a sign of life from Avery. His breath wheezed in and out.

Thank God. He was alive.

He leaned against the seat in front of him, his hand gripping it tight, blocking my view of his face. I shook his shoulder. "Are you okay?" I couldn't stop the way my heart was pounding in my chest, or the image in my mind of Avery doubling over.

He didn't answer and all eyes, except Hunter's, were on him. I ripped the case off Avery's chest and his backpack, then shoved them to the floor. "Avery." I pushed him back so I could see him better. He groaned, grabbing onto his chest.

"Move your hand," I demanded. I pushed it away, ripped off the Velcro to his bulletproof vest, then yanked it over his head. I moved my hands down his shirt; it was drenched in moisture. Fear gripped my chest and I pulled his shirt up, scared that I would see blood.

"He's okay." I sighed in relief. His chest was slick from sweat but he didn't even have a bruise. Both Easton and Hunter breathed out heavily.

Christian wrapped his hand around my arm and I turned to him. Gripping the front of my vest, he drug me to him and kissed me roughly. I grabbed his shoulders, clinging to him tight and feeling more alive than I'd ever felt before. Then he pulled away. "Are you okay?" His face was white and he kissed me again. "I thought he was going to shoot you in the head."

I nodded. "I'm okay."

"Shit." Hunter breathed out his relief and Easton gave me a dark look. Except for Easton, the tension in the car lowered as we flew down the street. Hunter looked in the rearview mirror and I turned to look behind us; no one was following.

"Give me your phones." Easton's voice came out a growl and he held out his hand. I slipped mine out of my pocket to hand over to him. He began taking out the batteries and sim cards. I slid back again and turned to Avery.

"Shit, Avery. I thought… I thought for a second when you leaned over…" I couldn't finish my sentence, remembering the fear that shot through my body when I thought he'd been shot.

He turned to me, his eyes burning into mine. His hands slid up my side and he pulled on my waist. I climbed into his lap, straddling him, staring back. His eyes were dark, intense, and trying to tell me something.

His hands went to the Velcro straps of my vest and loosened it. When it was off, he pulled me into him, wrapping his arms around me in a tight hug.

I sucked in a breath, surprised by his openness.

I breathed him in, his warmth, his arms around me. His heartbeat that was pounding in my ears. The way his fingers were trembling as they pulled through my hair. The real Avery.

Not the one hidden behind walls of stone to keep people from breaking his heart.

In that moment, that touch, open, vulnerable and giving, I knew the real him.

We sat like that for the whole car ride, me cradled in his lap and happy that he was alive. Him holding me like he was at the edge of a precipice and afraid to jump into the darkness.

6

When we pulled up, Avery hesitantly let me go and I slid back into my seat. He touched my cheek softly and then looked away. We were on a gravel driveway and the car slid to a stop. I peered through the window, taking in the dark and silent forest surrounding us.

Christian opened the door and I stepped out behind him, taking a moment to stretch my hands high over my head. I glanced nervously behind me and then turned towards the safe house. In the darkness, my wolf eyes took in the ramshackle cabin. The moonlight featured the hole in the bottom corner of the door.

I blinked my eyes. It was slightly leaning to the side.

It doesn't look like something from a horror movie. It doesn't look like something from a horror movie.

I took a deep breath, repeating the lie as I watched the guys walk to the back of the SUV.

"Grab my stuff, will you?" Avery's wall was back up, and the only other noise from him were his footsteps on the gavel.

I reached back in the SUV and grabbed the mask and strapped it on my back, then grabbed Avery's and my backpack. The guys took the rest of their equipment out of the trunk: a long black canvas bag that held our rifles, a couple of cases of bottled water, and another canvas bag with canned food and disposable phones.

Christian held his hand out to me and as I took it, he led me to the house. The door creaked as we entered and a mouse scurried through the room. I yelped as it dashed across the floor and disappeared through a hole in the wall. Hunter gave me a tired smile. "You're the baddest wolf this side of the continent and you're afraid of a mouse?"

I grinned. "That one had fangs, I swear."

He raised his eyebrow. "Next time, I'll spear him with a toothpick."

I swiped my arm at him, hitting him softly, and looked around. The cabin was one room, filled with three old mattresses on the floor. On the far side, there was a small kitchen with a narrow table, a sink and a gas stove. All of us in the cabin together made it seem very cramped. But, I honestly didn't give a shit how small it felt or how scary it looked because I was with my guys and we were all safe. I'd happily sleep on a concrete block at this point.

Hunter opened the bag and pulled out a disposable phone. Christian began taking cans out of the bag and I rushed to help him. We piled them up on the counter. There was a small desk next to a window, holding four old and yellowing tv screens. Easton turned them on, checking to see if the video feeds covering the woods were still working. He unpacked his computer and opened it, sitting in the folding chair. His face held a scowl, like he was pissed off at something.

Avery sunk to one of the mattresses and leaned his head against the wall. He closed his eyes, his face a blank mask. I thought about going to him, I wanted to hold him again, to know that he was really real and alive and breathing. But I held off, deciding that he needed some space.

Nobody said anything, but Easton, Hunter, and Christian kept glancing at me. Done with the cans, I looked around the room, looking for a safe spot to put the mask. Their eyes followed me as I put the case on the kitchen table. I knew we were all thinking the same thing. That guy wasn't with the army. He was sent there specifically to kill me.

I had to face the facts. Someone was seriously trying to kill me and one of these days, they weren't going to miss. Our mission just got more complicated. Somehow they knew we were there. They wanted the artifact and they wanted me dead. And, they had access to some serious killing machines to accomplish their goals.

"Is there a bathroom?" I needed a second to just think without their eyes on me. Christian pointed towards the corner and I noticed the door. Except for Avery, all eyes stayed with me as I strode across the room, jumping over the mattresses. When I reached it, Christian started taking off his uniform. "I'm going outside. I'll fly up, check the roads and the woods."

Hunter nodded. Easton stood up, looking at Christian. "Check camera four, the one at the entrance to the driveway. Something's blocking it. Looks like a branch."

Christian nodded and, butt-naked, strode out the front door.

I watched him go, then opened the door to the bathroom cautiously, my eyes scanning the floor for any more animals. Once I was sure there was nothing furry scurrying across the floor, I stepped inside. The sink was a pale yellow color and had a rust ring around the drain. I grasped the handle to the cold water; it was rough against my hand. I held it there for a minute, trying to steady my shaking hand. Then I turned the handle.

The pipes made a shooting, spraying noise and it took a second before brown water spurt into the sink.

I heard Easton moving the table; it scraped as he pushed it across the wooden floor. Then Hunter spoke. "I need to speak to Liam." The room was silent, then he spoke again. "Yes." Another pause. "We're safe. We'll be waiting for his call."

Once the water was clear, I cupped my hands under it. It was cold and the shock of it felt good against my skin. I splashed my face and ran my hands through my hair, looking in the mirror. It was a dull silver and spotted in the corner with age and neglect. I tried to relax, but adrenaline burned through my veins. It hummed like a song, vibrating and pulsing through me.

We were in so much fucking trouble. How were we going to keep safe and help Aria at the same time? I had a target on me; we were going to have to figure out who was trying to kill me now. There was no way around it.

"Screw it." Easton's dark voice from across the room made me shiver. His steps were heavy as he tromped towards the bathroom and then he appeared behind me, his face determined. He stepped into the room, crowding me in, and slammed the door behind me.

I swiveled around to face him and he pushed me back and up against the wall. Then his lips were on mine, his hands all over me. "I couldn't reach you in time." His lips moved to my throat. "I saw him aiming the gun and I fucking knew he was here for you." Leaning lower, he bit my shoulder. "Thank God for Avery."

His hands went to my shirt. He whipped it off and dropped it to the floor. My heart hammered, imagining him ramming into me. I grabbed his pants and fumbled open the button, needing to feel him in my hands. He groaned as I took his throbbing dick, stroking it up and down. My whole body responded, lighting my senses on fire.

His expression was dark and he growled as his thumbs pressed against my collar, digging into my skin. "I need to be inside you, now."

He yanked my pants off and guided his dick inside me, pinning me under him. Then he pounded into me, hitting me against the wall as his dick filled me. Our pubic bones smashed against each other as he slammed his hips roughly, and I gripped his shoulders to push him in deeper.

I felt so alive, so aroused. I needed him to fuck me with everything he had. I groaned, not caring that the rest of the guys could probably hear us. But he slapped his hand over my lips and I scraped my teeth against his palm.

He stared into my eyes, his dick thick and firm inside me. "Be a quiet little wolf and I'll eat your pussy."

I stared back at him, eyes wide and my breath quickening at the thought.

"You want me to eat your cunt, don't you?"

I nodded and slipped my tongue out to touch his hand. He bit his lips, trying to keep his own growl in. "Just give me a minute first."

I nodded and, keeping his hand over my mouth, he slammed into me again. He closed his eyes, shifting his hips to bury into me deeper. I gripped his ass, wrapping one of my legs around him, loving the way he felt inside me. Fuck, fuck, he felt so good. His hand slipped off my mouth to grip my hips as his thrusts turned harsher.

Then he suddenly stopped and pulled out of me. He turned me around to face the wall and smacked his hand against my ass. I inhaled a breath as electricity shot up into my cunt.

"You're so fucking naughty. Fucking me with the rest of the guys only a thin wall between us."

He smacked my ass again. "You like that don't you?"

I nodded, holding in my moan. He took a step back and rubbed the spot where he'd hit. "Get on the sink."

Knees, trembling, I scrambled to the sink. He thrust my knees apart and I leaned back on both my hands, waiting with trembling anticipation for his touch. His tongue, wet and rough, moved up my inner thigh as his hands pressed my knees even further apart. I panted, wanting, needing more. He bit my pussy lip and I jerked forward. He clasped his hand on my stomach, holding me still as his teeth roughly worked higher to my clit, scraping across it roughly.

I bit down on my response, as he lapped me with his tongue. My mouth fell open as prickling sensations shot through my body. I gasped in air, trying to contain the groan that wanted to slip from my mouth.

"That's it. Keep quiet."

"More." I whispered. "I need more, Easton."

His fingers entered me and I ground against his face roughly, my orgasm building rapidly.

"That's right, my good little wolf. Take what you need from me."

He moved his fingers in and out, his tongue lapped at my pussy and all I could do was just feel as my orgasm shot through me. It was sharp and pulled at my stomach, causing small spasms to rock through my body.

The second I relaxed, he yanked me off the sink and slammed me against the wall, pounding into me again.

"Fuck. I need to fuck you," was all he could say as he filled me up, his hands grabbing mine to hold them over my head. His thrusts grew more frantic and I ground my hips against him. Then he grunted, emptying himself into me.

I cursed, loving the way his cum slipped in between my legs, claiming me possessively. I loved the feel of his rough hands on me. The way his fingers turned from controlling to gentle as they moved down my arms to my side. I leaned forward to nip at his lips, biting them softly and a shudder ran through his body. He grinned, meeting my eyes.

"Fuck, babe."

I grinned back. All the adrenaline running through my body had been burned, pushed, fucked out.

Then his face grew serious. "Don't ever die. It would kill me. It would kill us."

I nodded. "You guys, too. I don't know what would've happened if…" I still couldn't say it, couldn't think of what would've happened…

He grabbed some clean toilet paper from under the sink and handed me some. "Speaking of the guys." He cleaned himself and buttoned up his pants. "We need to talk. Everyone together. The tension is getting too thick between us. And Avery, he…"

I put my hand against his mouth and he looked at me, reading me. I pulled him close and he wrapped his arms around me. I sighed and leaned into him. I just needed to feel him for a moment.

We stood there in silence and I took in a deep breath, calming my troubled heart. He didn't say anything else for a while; he just let me hold him. I pressed my head against his chest, listening to the beat of his heart, wishing I could hold it in my hand, keep it close. He rubbed my back then moved his hands down to my ass and lifted me up. He gently sat me on the sink again.

He softly pulled my chin up. "Lizzy, look at me."

I looked into his eyes and his gaze darkened. "Damn, woman. I can't stand the way you look at me sometimes. I just want to bend you over and fuck you again."

I bit my lip and noticed that he was getting hard again.

He closed his eyes, gripping my thighs, then he opened my legs and stood in between them. Gently tugging, he pulled my sports bra over my head then he traced his fingers down to my breasts, fondling them softly. Goosebumps broke out over my skin and I scooted closer to the edge of the sink, wanting to be near him. He stared at my boobs as his thumbs raked over the hardened tips, worshipping them with his touch. His fingers moved higher, up over my shoulders and up my neck. They stopped at my jaw and he tugged my head up to make me look into his eyes. "Lizzy, what is it that you want?"

His other hand trailed back down my body, in between my breasts and down to my bare pussy. "If you could have anything, what would it be?"

His fingers parted my outer lips, and he ran his finger through it. It was slippery with his cum. I moved my hips slowly, wanting more, taking in the sensations as he played with me.

"Lizzy." His voice was dark and it made me shiver. "Tell me."

"All of you."

He leaned down to scrape his teeth against my ear. "All of us?"

I nodded, reveling in the sensations coursing through my body as his fingers worked me over again. Fuck, I needed to come again.

"I want you all. I can't give any of you up."

His breath moved over me. "Then why haven't you told us yet?"

"It's because—" My breath caught as he inserted two fingers inside me.

"Keep going baby, and I'll make you come again."

"I can't tell anyone yet, because of Christian."

He paused for a second, and then his thumb found my nub. He pressed it softly. "And why because of Christian?"

I couldn't think, I couldn't breathe, all I could think of was how I wanted him to touch me, to play with me. I moved my hips, strained against him but he held back, giving me a second to think.

"It's cuz..." I took in a deep breath. "It's cuz he doesn't want to share."

Easton stilled. "What?"

I opened my eyes.

"He told you that?" He moved his hand again, pressing against my clit.

I licked my lips. "Yes." I breathed heavily. "Yes." Shit, it felt so good.

"Lizzy?"

"Hmm?"

He raked his stubble against my cheek. "Remember how I told you that if you were going to choose us all, that you needed to have sex with all of us?"

"Yes." My voice betrayed my want. "I want to fuck you all, but I just... I just don't know how. I mean, Avery won't even look at me again and Christian, I don't want to hurt him."

I closed my eyes as his thumb pressed tighter against my clit. I rubbed myself against his hand. "Shit, Easton, don't stop."

"Keeping the team together and happy is important to me. We need each other. You need to fuck us all to make that happen."

I nodded. "Okay, yes. I want to."

"Avery will work it out. He just needs some time. And Christian, I think if you give him a taste of your pussy, he won't be able to turn you down."

"I'm not a whore, Easton." I opened my eyes to see his smoldering gaze on me.

"That's right. You're not a whore." His voice was firm. "You belong to us. And only us." He flicked my clit and I cried out, then he pushed his fingers in deeper, while rubbing against my clit, making my orgasm come to a head. I gripped his arms, leaning against his hold and convulsing.

He held me close. "You are ours. Only, you haven't claimed us. So do it, Lizzy. Take what we're offering you. Fuck Christian and fuck Avery. Let them taste what Hunter and I have. Show them how much you want them."

I nodded, feeling warm in the afterglow of my orgasm. Then I put my feet on the ground, feeling his cum slide down my thighs. He watched me carefully as I stood and reached for the door, a smirk on my face.

He grabbed my hand. "Where are you going like that?"

"To go offer Christian my pussy."

He growled, pulling me to him before I could open the door and I laughed.

"Not right now, you aren't. Right now, you're mine. Just one moment longer." He nuzzled into my neck, kissing it softly, pressing me against the wall again. "Besides, Christian's not here, remember?"

We could hear Hunter and Avery talking through the door. I opened my mouth to speak but Easton put his hand over my mouth. "Shh…"

I looked at the door, like I could see through it. Easton swiveled around so that we were leaning against the door. There was a pause, and then Hunter spoke again.

"That's not the only thing I regret."

I froze, and Easton's hands gripped me harder. What the hell were they talking about?

I took in a breath, pressing closer to the door to listen in.

§

"No. Don't do this." Avery's voice was hard, tortured.

"But it's my fault. It's my fault they brought you onto the team. It's my fault they turned you into this." Hunter burst this out like his confession had been eating him alive. I snuggled deeper into Easton, needing the contact. I felt a pang at Hunter's voice. I'd never heard him so raw, so emotional and, it ate me up inside. I looked at Easton and whispered. "Hunter brought Avery on to the team?"

Easton nodded, gripping me tight. "He was the only one not chosen by Sophia."

"Stop, Hunter. Don't say that."

"Sophia didn't want to bring you in, but I insisted. Maybe if I'd left you in the hospital that day, you wouldn't be here with us. You'd be living a better life, probably with a family by now."

"You're so full of shit. This isn't on you. My choices aren't on your back. I decided to join the team, to be what I am. And only I can answer for my sins."

Hunter growled. "We all have to answer for our sins. For the things we've done. And bringing you on is one of mine."

Avery was silent and I could hear Hunter begin to pace. Finally, Avery spoke and his voice was so quiet I had to strain to hear him.

"Hunter, you think that bringing me on was the wrong choice but in all reality, you saved me."

What?

Hunter stopped pacing. "Don't lie to me."

"I'm not. I know that I struggle to deal with my... job. But doing this job, at that time, when Mia died and I had nothing left in the world? This job is what kept me sane. It gave me a mission, a purpose in life. It kept me from giving in when all I wanted was to let the darkness swallow me whole. And I still miss her. God, I miss Mia so much sometimes. I can't help it."

I felt a trace of jealousy for the woman he loved. Would he ever feel that way about me? Did I even have a right to ask him for that? To ask him to rip out his beating heart and hand it over to me, when at the same time I couldn't give up the rest of my guys?

"But this job gave me something to focus on. And eventually, it brought Lizzy to me. It brought the only woman I've ever wanted since Mia. And even having that hope that she could love me... That fleeting hope, a whisper of a promise that I can love again and be loved in return, it means everything to me."

My stomach churned and Easton stroked my stomach with his thumb. So Avery did still want me.

He continued. "So don't you dare say that my life would be better without this job. I would've died if it wasn't for you, okay? And don't you motherfucking act like you're my grim reaper, because you're not. You're my savior, okay?"

I was stunned and apparently so was Hunter because he didn't answer. And yet, I felt a bit of hope spark. I wanted to burst in the room, tell him I did love him. Give him my undying devotion. Force Avery to talk to me. To tell me what the fuck was going on. If he wanted me so much, why was he trying to leave?

But Easton's grip tightened on me, as if he could read my mind.

"No, Lizzy, now isn't the time. Let Hunter open him up. Let them work this out, this has been between them since before you got here."

I opened my mouth to argue but decided against it. He was right. I wasn't the center of this issue between them. I nodded, agreeing.

The room grew quiet and Easton ran his nose up my neck, taking in a deep breath. "You smell like me." I flushed, and his hands fell on my hips. He pulled me around to face him. "Take a shower. I'll wait a few minutes to let them finish, then leave." His eyes darkened. "Remember what I told you. Right now, Avery's acting like an ass, but he just needs to know that you still care about him. We'll get this straightened out."

I nodded and he turned me towards the shower. "Now get clean." He slapped my ass and I jumped. I turned back around, grinning.

"Next time you do that, you'd better be ready to fucking take me again, cuz that is hot as hell."

I saw his eyes darken, but I turned the water on, and waited for it to warm up.

❧

THE SHOWER WAS REFRESHING BUT I RUSHED THROUGH IT. FINDING AN old hand towel under the sink, I dried myself off. I made sure to get every drop, because it was going to be hella hard to get my uniform on if I was still wet.

I stilled as Christian's voice came through the door. "Should we tell her?"

Then Hunter spoke. "We have to, the Queen trusted her with this." So I was the she. I grabbed my uniform and peeled it back on; it was faster now that I knew how to do it.

Easton's voice was angry. "She's not responsible for what happened. The Queen obviously has a leak."

"Andre did this. The men were too prepared, they had military grade weaponry. They had a fucking tank, for hell's sake." Hunter was angry too. "But how did he find out about it? Maybe one of the soldiers in her inner circle?"

I opened the door. "What's going on?"

Avery was sitting by the window next to the monitors, holding a rifle and keeping an eye on the woods beyond us. Christian was sitting at the table, back from checking the woods, and Easton and Hunter were crowded around him. Their eyes were on me as I crossed the room.

They had the same look on their faces. Fear.

"What?" A nervousness slithered through my stomach. "Somebody tell me what happened."

Hunter moved to the side and I slipped in between him and Easton. The case for the mask was open and the mask was shattered into five large pieces. Careful not to disturb the mask, I flipped the lid over. The bullet had pierced it, just enough to shatter the mask; it was still embedded into the cover.

"I thought the case was bulletproof."

Hunter crossed his arms across his chest. "It is."

I frowned. "What kind of bullet is this?" I reached for it.

"Stop!" Two sets of arms grabbed for me, pulling me back and Christian jerked the cover away.

"Don't touch it. It could be poisoned. Or have a magic spell of some sort. That's why we haven't taken it out."

I glanced at Avery, who hadn't moved from his lookout spot and swallowed hard. "Would this bullet have pierced his vest?"

The room was quiet but Easton and Hunter nodded. A shiver ran up my spine. Hunter gripped my hand and Christian gently closed the case, avoiding the bullet, and slid it back in the bag. I looked at Hunter and caught the look between him and Easton.

"Is Avery okay?"

Hunter rubbed my arm, brushing off my concern. "He's fine, this isn't near the closest he's come to death."

"Avery still has ears, you know." Avery's voice was angry and rough.

"He does? I thought they were shot off."

He peeked at me, his face turning back into his familiar scowl. "No, they still work. I can hear everything."

I knew he was talking about Easton and me.

I crossed my arms, giving him an inviting look. "Too bad you didn't join us."

He scowled and I stuck my tongue out. He rolled his eyes and I sighed. I'd have to work harder to get a reaction out of him.

"I think the Queen needs to know about this." Christian's comment made me turn back to the mask. He faced me, a sympathetic look on his face. Hunter pulled me to him and put his arm around my waist protectively.

I leaned into him, loving being around my guys. Loving the way they looked at me, the way they touched me. I was so fucking lucky.

"I think she already knows."

"How?" Easton was being protective too and I was so confused. Why were they being so weird?

"I think she can..." I tried to explain. "Feel it. It affects her magic when this happens. She'll have known that we were on our mission tonight and would be paying attention to it."

Easton grabbed my arm, pulling me away from Hunter to face me. His eyes intently stared into mine and his eyebrows drew in. "You're not taking the fall for this. You're not sacrificing us again to fix this."

Understanding washed over me. Ohhh. That's why they were being so protective. Christian stood up and gripped my arm tight. "We won't let it happen. I don't care about the relic."

"Christian." I frowned. "Of course, we have to fix this." I knew the minute I saw it that I could fix it. But I hadn't thought about what the guys would think.

"What? You think I don't have strong feelings for you, Pinky?" He stepped closer and I was now in the middle of the three guys. "Do you think I don't think of you in the night, wishing you were in my arms? That I don't want you as badly as the rest of the team?" His finger traced my cheek softly but his eyes were fierce and intense.

Easton was right. I needed to address the tension that was building between us.

"No." I shook my head. "I know you care for me."

Out of the corner of my eye I saw Avery looking at us and I felt an overwhelming pressure on my chest. It was too much. There was too much attention on me. I looked around the room. It was so small, too small.

"Hunter, can I have a phone, please?" My voice came out a squeak.

He reached in his pocket and pulled out the phone. I took it and slipped through the circle of men crowding me. "Did Liam call yet?"

Hunter shook his head and I grabbed Christian's arm. "I'm going outside to call him, and Christian," I dragged him across the room. "You're coming with me. We can fix this, but I want to talk to him first."

a s soon as we were outside, I took in a deep breath, smelling the scent that comes with the forest and it eased the tension in my shoulders. The door closed behind me with a click and silence settled around us. The moonlight filtered through the trees, casting a soft glow over the landscape. The sun would be up in a few hours. But the coolness of the night didn't stop the snow from melting. Water dripped from the trees with a trickling sound.

I looked up at Christian, who stared at me with a troubled look on his face. Ignoring it, I punched in Liam's private number. Then I pulled Christian to me and leaned against the cabin.

Liam answered after the first ring. "Sorry I didn't call you back. I was just dealing with… other issues. Tell me what happened."

"Someone knew we were there."

"Shit."

"They came in military uniforms, with a tank."

"What the hell?"

I heard noises in the background, like he was looking through a desk. "Do you have the artifact?"

"Yes, but it's broken." He was silent for a moment. A pulse of warmth flooded me and I traced my fingers over Christian's chest. His hands were on my hips and he rubbed his lips over my forehead.

"There's one more thing. There was someone else, using armor-piercing bullets. He almost killed Avery."

"Is everyone okay?"

I took in a breath. "Yeah. You should know though, he was aiming for me. Avery jumped in front of me." Christian's arms around me tightened. "If he hadn't had the relic strapped to his chest, he would've been hit."

"What about the bullet? Anything special about it?"

"We're not sure if it's spelled or poisoned or anything."

"Get it to Edward, he'll be able to check it out."

"Liam. You know Aria has a problem right?"

"Of course I know that." His voice was tight, controlled, and I felt bad that my words came out as harsh as they did. I tried to soften my tone.

"Look, this actually will help us. Now we know that it's deeper than Aria thought. Who else knew about the mission?"

He was quiet and I imagined he was facing some tough questions. Had they told anyone they really trusted? When he responded, his voice was low.

"I'll look into this. In the meantime, I'll check Aria's rooms for any magical bugging spells. There could be other ways that Andre found out, if it's him. He has access to the deepest resources. Plus I heard that he's been involving himself with witches who use black magic." He paused. "Or he could've just had someone watching the museum. Were they waiting for you?"

"No, they came about eight minutes in."

"It's a possibility then. Although eight minutes is really fast to put together such a strong force of men. Too fast for a tank."

"We'll approach him directly, ask him if he's involved. It may draw him out."

"I'll set it up. But be careful." He took in a deep breath. "Elizabeth, very few people knew about this mission."

I thought about that. At this point, there were only a few people I could trust. And one of them was standing next to me. Christian pulled my hair over my ear and I looked up at him. He kissed my forehead.

"I trust you to figure it out, Liam. I'm putting my life in your hands."

He was silent for a moment, then he responded. "You can count on me. I'll set up an appointment with you to see Andre in two days. Stay out of sight until then, and I'll work on my end to figure out what happened. If you leave any earlier, let me know."

I nodded, even though he couldn't see me. "Yes, sir."

"And the artifact? You know how to fix it, right?"

"I think so."

"Good." His voice grew light. "You should be able to handle that now, no problem."

"That's right. Cuz I'm a badass."

He laughed. "You are a badass." I heard another voice in the background and it sounded like he put his hand over the speaker. After a moment, he spoke. "I gotta run. I'll call you on this number if I need you." Then the line was dead.

"Well goodbye to you, too."

Christian chuckled and I slipped the phone into my pocket, then put my arms around his waist and looked up at him.

"What do you think?"

His face grew serious. "I think I'm glad you're still alive. It was touch and go for a moment." He stepped forward, pushing me with him, my back against the cabin. "Pinky, what are you doing to me? Why do you torture me so much? Why don't you just rip the Band-Aid off?" His lips moved over my lips, to my neck, by my collar.

"Christian, I..." My mouth was suddenly dry. I knew I should say something to him, but all I could do was feel the way my nerves tingled every time his lips brushed mine, feel the warmth that traveled up my chest as his fingers inched higher up my side. My heart pounded and I clutched his shirt. Wanting to kiss him, wanting to taste him on my lips. Wanting to feel his naked skin over mine. I didn't care that I'd just had sex with Easton, or that I wanted to be with all of them, all of the time. They were mine and I wouldn't accept anything less.

He stopped kissing me to look into my eyes. "What do you want, Pinky?"

The same words that Easton spoke, the words that kept everything either in balance or turned everything upside down.

He gripped my jaw and his lips encased mine. His kiss was harsh. Like he was tired of waiting for me to come to him. Like he couldn't wait another moment. It was demanding and possessive.

"Because I want you, Pinky. I want to feel your hands over me, touching me in ways that no one has ever touched." He stepped back and turned me around so that my stomach pressed against the cabin. His mouth went to my ear. "I want to feel your naked body against mine as I make love to you. To feel your silky, soft skin as I run my lips over your breasts, your stomach. Your pussy."

Shit. I sucked in a breath.

His hands moved my hair over my shoulder and his lips moved over the back of my neck. He bit it gently, sending a thrill through my chest. "I want to fill you up, to make you moan my name over and over."

Heat ran through my body and every sensation was on fire. "Christian."

My body was in overdrive, my hormones raging. I wanted this. I wanted everything he offered and more. I wanted all of him, every day.

"I want to make pancakes for you in the morning and sing to you in the shower. To have little Christian babies running around." His hands cupped me and my mouth parted as his fingers traced the front of my pants. Moaning, I pressed against his hand, smelling the pine and dirt as I took in every sensation. His other hand wrapped around my stomach, holding me close as he tortured me with his touch, tickling me through the material.

Then he yanked me around again, kissing me passionately. I wrapped my hands around his neck, clinging to him tightly. Kissing him, loving him, pressing against him, moaning his name.

"Please, Christian." I begged him with my words, my lips. Begged him to take me.

He pulled back sharply, staring into my eyes. "What the fuck do you want, Lizzy? Tell me."

"I want you, Christian. You know that. I want everything you said and more. But you know that I can't give up the other guys."

He sucked in a breath and I felt a prickling sensation around my waist, where his hands were. He tried to pull away but I gripped him tighter. "Can't you see, Christian? I need you. I need all of you." Biting my lip, I ran my hand over his chest. "Each one of you mean so much to me, I can't let you go, any of you."

He didn't answer, but only stared over my shoulder. Silence settled around us. The only sounds were the small animals in the woods behind us and it killed me that he was suffering. But I couldn't let him go.

I stood on my tiptoes, brushing my lips across his. "Please, Christian. I don't want to loose you."

He sighed and leaned his forehead on the top of my head. "Just give me some time. I need time to think, to accept this. It's just not what I had planned for my life."

"What about when you were all with Sophia?"

He frowned. "Things were different with her. We didn't actually love her. Plus, we all thought we were saving the race."

I nodded. "Your sense of honor is one reason why I love you all so much. And who's to say that we can't have all those things that you want? Just in a different way, with all of us. Together."

He took my face in his hands, staring at me intently. "This is what you want? You want me?"

I nodded. "Yes. You are part of us. A part of me. I love you, Christian. I need you by my side."

He pulled me to him. "Okay. Just give me some time then, okay?"

I nodded and held him close, wishing I could be everything to every guy. How could I show him how much he meant to me? I was beginning to feel like I was falling short. Could I really do this? Make every single one of them feel loved? Could I give them enough? Be enough for them?

His hands moved down my side, then they clutched my hands. "Should we go in?"

I nodded. "Sure."

He took in a deep breath and we stepped up to the screen door.

"How are you going to fix the artifact?"

Grinning, I eyed him. "This badass will think of something."

☙

THE SMELL OF RAVIOLI FILLED MY NOSE AS WE CAME INSIDE THE CABIN. Avery was at the table and Easton was keeping an eye on the video monitors; they were both eating out of cups. Hunter leaned against the counter, eating out of the pan.

"Your food's there." He pointed to two bowls, overflowing with the tomatoed pasta. "Water's in the fridge."

My stomach growled and I made a bee-line for the counter, tugging Christian with me.

Christian took his cup of ravioli and looked at the counter. There was only one fork. Shrugging, he left it for me and sat next to Avery at the rickety table. Instead of digging into the food, I opened the fridge and gulped down a bottle of water. Feeling better, I stood next to Hunter.

"No more bowls?" I nodded at the pan.

"Yeah." He grinned and warmth washed over me. I loved his smile. He leaned down and kissed me. His eyes stared into mine and I couldn't stop my smile. Then he pinched my cheek softly and began eating again. I grabbed the bowl of pasta and leaned against the counter.

"Everything looks good, but I'll go out in a minute and take one more look, see if anyone's around before we sleep." Easton got up and washed his bowl. After he put it back in the cupboard, he leaned against the counter and guided me to stand in between his legs. I leaned against his chest, feeling warm and soft inside.

Avery reached over and speared one of Christian's ravioli's. Christian tipped the cup towards Avery who, after shoving the ravioli in his mouth, speared two more.

"Thanks, man," Avery managed to say in between bites.

Christian nodded then pushed back his chair and, putting his feet up on the table, began to eat. "Lizzy's going to tell us how to fix the mask without killing us." All eyes turned towards me, catching me in the middle of a yawn. I gave Christian a look but he just winked at me, eating his ravioli with his fingers.

I put my cup on the table and took in a deep breath. "Sure. But I think we should do it over there." I pointed to the mattress.

Easton spoke up. "Just let her eat first."

Hunter put the empty pan on the stove, then wrapped his arm around my waist and pulled me in front of him. Easton let me go and I was switched back again from Easton to Hunter, who gave me back my bowl. "Eat first, Princess, then we sleep. Tomorrow, you can work your magic. The mask can wait a day."

"Thanks." I really was hungry. I leaned back into him, loving the way he felt. He held me tight and I watched Avery eat. He ignored me. I continued to stare at him, hoping to get a reaction out of him. When he didn't look over, I threw one of my ravioli's at him and it landed on his cheek.

He caught it and, still not looking at me, put his hand in his lap. I watched him closely, annoyed that after everything, he was still being an ass. He squeezed the ravioli tight and the mash of tomato sauce and meat slid between his fingers.

I sighed, wondering what the hell I would have to do to get him to act normal again.

After the kitchen was cleaned, Easton left to fly over the woods and we began to settle for the night.

"Pinky."

I turned towards Christian, yawning again. I was so ready to crash. "What's up?"

"Which blanket do you want? The pink one with the hole, or the blue one with the hole?" He held up two blue moth-eaten blankets and one pink one. I pointed to the blue ones.

He grinned. "We'll give Avery the pink one."

I smiled. "Sounds perfect." Avery was in the shower. He was the last one and I was pretty sure the cloth I'd used to dry off was soaking wet by now.

"Pick a mattress."

There were only three mattresses and I picked the one in the middle, wanting to be near all my guys. As soon as I lay down, Christian crawled up in the one next to me. He put our blanket around us and I snuggled into him. The water to Avery's shower turned off and I considered telling him he could use his blanket to dry off. I yawned again. Nah, then he'd just be wet all night long.

Hunter kicked at the mattress next to mine, pushing it towards me. Then he lay down and pressed into my back. He wrapped his arms around me and I was sandwiched in between the two. Easton was going to take first watch and everyone was going to take turns. I barely heard Avery come out of the bathroom before I passed out.

❧

I WOKE WITH THE SUN IN MY FACE; IT WAS WELL INTO MID-DAY AND everyone was up except for me. I sat up, realizing that someone forgot to wake me for my turn to take the watch. Grumpily, I got up and stomped off the mattress, kicking the blankets to the floor. I was part of the team damnit, I needed to help out as much as them. I wanted to keep us all safe, too.

We didn't eat ravioli for breakfast; it was SpaghettiOs instead. The breakfast of champions. It did make me feel better, though. I sat on Christian's lap at the table, trying to figure out a way to get them back. After we ate, we cleaned up and then the guys all gravitated towards me.

It was show time.

"Easton, will you bring the mask?"

We sat in a circle on the middle mattress, and it reminded me of when we fixed the magic book. Except this time, I had an idea of what I was doing.

"Sit with your knees touching each other." I chuckled to myself as they shuffled closer together. "Now, hold hands."

Their eyes went to me.

"Seriously?" Easton looked at Hunter like he had the chicken pox.

"What? You guys are touching each other all the time. And now you can't hold hands?" I nodded my head towards the mask. "Not to fix the mask? Not to save our bond?"

I was really pushing it but this was fun. Grumbling, they took each other's hands and I stifled my laugh. "Now, each of you close your eyes and repeat after me."

I waited and, after a hesitation, they all closed their eyes. A warmth washed over me and suddenly I felt a little bit guilty. They held a lot of trust in me, and here I was, using it to poke fun at them. Shoving my guilt aside, I began.

"I solemnly swear." I stopped, waiting for them to begin.

"I solemnly swear," their deep male voices reverberated throughout the room and it made me feel their strength, their power. Easton, who was sitting across from me, peeked through one eye.

"That I'm up to no good." I was really trying to hold in my laughter now.

"That I'm..." Varying voices repeated after me, each stopping once they realized that I was fucking with them. Hunter, who had watched my face grow red from trying to keep my laugh in, vaulted over the mask, tackling me.

"What the?" Christian's serious voice sounded so confused as Hunter rolled over into Avery's lap. Avery shoved us onto the floor and Christian joined Hunter in dog piling me.

"Help! Eastie." I was on my back, with Christian and Hunter on top of me. I threw my hand out to Easton but he just folded his arms over his chest, doing absolutely nothing to help. "Come on!" I cried out, trying to squirm out from under them. Then Easton joined them, stretching out over my thighs with a grin.

"You think I don't know a Harry Potter reference when I hear one?"

"But still, you're supposed to be on my side!" I managed to inch my way towards the edge of the mattress and squealed as they grappled at my legs, holding me still.

I gasped out, trying to catch my breath. "Avery!"

He eyed me warily, looking so serious.

I held my hand out. "Come on, man!"

He leaned forward, his face looming over me. His eyes were serious, so serious, as he stared at me. Then, he clasped my chin and kissed me.

I froze in shock. I was absolutely not expecting that.

His tongue forced my lips open and then his beard was prickling my skin as he poured all of his passion into his kiss. I clasped his face, deepening the kiss. Then he pulled back, his eyes closed, and rubbed my nose with his.

I couldn't move, I was pinned down by all the guys. I tried to kiss him again. He opened his eyes revealing pain and agony and anger, swirling and twisting in that look. An ache pounded in my chest.

Then he sat back and got to his feet.

"Get off, get off." I yelled at the guys, trying to make them hurry. Avery was going to bolt, I just knew it.

Avery gracefully jumped over mattresses, pulling his uniform shirt off. He was going to shift as soon as he got to the door and fly away.

I couldn't let that happen. I had to stop him.

"Avery, wait."

Easton pushed me up and forward, and I leapt across the room. "Stop!"

Avery's hand was on the door, his face determined. Fear welled in my chest, pushing upwards through my chest and choking off my air. I was only a second behind him but I was going to be too late. Scales rippled over his arms and he was halfway out the door.

I cried out, desperate. "Why do you hate me so much?" Tears sparked in my eyes and all the emotion and fear I'd been pushing down broke to the surface. It didn't make sense, he acted like he loved me. He'd risked his life to save mine. But what did he really feel for me, to be able to just walk away from me? From us? He didn't trust me to tell me the truth. Didn't that mean that he didn't love me? Not really?

He froze, halfway in, halfway out the door. He was breathing great puffing breaths in and out, still indecisive if he was going to bolt.

"What have I done to you to make you want to run away from me so bad?" I was close to the door now, torn between getting on my knees and begging him to stay or reaching out to grab him to physically force him to stay. Except I couldn't do that. He had to make the choice now. We'd delayed him long enough.

The rest of the guys had rushed to their feet but now they were still, and you could hear a pin drop in the room.

Avery swiveled towards me, his face a mask of anger. "What the hell makes you think this is about you? Maybe I just don't want you, Elizabeth."

His words shot daggers through my heart but I gripped my hands into fists at my side, determined to force him to face the truth. "I don't believe that. I know you're lying to me."

"You are so self-centered, so selfish. You think the whole world revolves around you. Get it through your thick head. I don't love you. And I can't stand to be around the team anymore. We're constantly distracted by you."

"Avery, enough." Hunter strode to my side and put his arms around me. "Quit being such as ass." Hunter pulled me into him, his warmth surrounding me as Avery attacked me again, pointing at me.

"You are the one breaking us up. It's your fault that we can't work together anymore. You're nothing but a self-centered—"

"I've had enough of this shit. Quit putting your issues on her. She's not Mia."

I sucked in a breath.

Avery stumbled back, taken off guard. He clasped the door frame, breathing heavily. His eyes narrowed at Easton, then he launched himself forward. "Don't you dare mention her name like that."

Easton sidestepped out of the way, then pushed Avery forward, launching him across the room. Avery flew to the floor, sliding across it and crashed into the table. Growling, he got to his feet, his nose bleeding. "What the hell, Easton?" He charged again, his wings extending from his back as he launched himself at Easton again.

"No!" I jumped forward, pulling myself out of Hunter's arms, just as Avery crashed into Easton. They both tumbled to the floor. Avery landed on top and punched Easton in the chest. Blood was dripping from Avery's nose all over Easton. Easton smacked Avery's nose with the heel of his hand.

Avery howled, holding his nose. He fell, landing on his side and crumpling his wings. All the fight drained out of him in exchange for the pain in his nose. Easton didn't move, just laid on his back, breathing heavily.

I stood over them, filled with such agony. What Avery said was right. I was breaking up the team. I couldn't do this anymore. I had to do something, anything.

But I needed to know something first.

I held out both my hands, an offering. Easton used it to pull himself up but Avery ignored my offer. He stood up, staring at me, clutching at his broken nose. The look of rage he was giving me was so hateful, so spiteful. It was like he really did hate me.

I folded my arms. "Tell me the truth, Avery. Look into my eyes and tell me you don't love me. Tell me you want to break the bond with me and I'll let you go. I'll sign the paperwork. If," my voice caught, "If this is what you really want, I'll let you go."

He looked into my eyes and opened his mouth to answer. Every part of my body was taut, filled with tension. Afraid of what he was going to say. "I don't hate you Lizzy but…" His face hardened, his burnt-sienna eyes turned to cold steel. "But I don't love you."

His words slammed into me and I felt a crushing weight, but I held his gaze. "Fine. I'll sign the paperwork as soon as we get back."

"Avery." Christian's voice cut through us. He wasn't angry, his voice was soft even.

"What?" Avery's voice was vicious, a stark contrast to Christian's.

Christian folded his arms across his broad chest. "You have to tell her the truth."

"She thinks she wants to know, but she doesn't. Not really." Avery's nose was crooked and it was beginning to mend.

"I want to know." Easton pressed into my side, giving Avery the evil eye.

Faster than I believed was possible, Christian reached out and grabbed Avery's nose, straightening it. It made a loud crunching noise and I winced. Avery sucked in a breath but now it would heal back straight.

"It doesn't matter." Christian continued as if nothing had happened. "She deserves to know the truth."

Avery exploded. "Why? Why does she have to know? I need to fix this first, before I tell her."

Christian frowned. "You can't fix this by yourself Avery. It's bigger than just one of us."

Avery took in a breath to argue but Christian shook his head, interrupting him. "You need to face the truth, Avery. It's not about her at all, is it?"

Avery didn't speak, he just stared at Christian, his mouth open. Hunter and Easton were growing restless but my heart was hammering in my chest. What was it? I wanted to run to him, to shake him, to make him just spit it out.

Christian touched Avery's arm. "Tell her. We'll make her understand."

Avery clenched his hands into fists, breathing in and out as he stared at Christian. Christian's hand was still on Avery's arm and I saw Avery soften. Christian was helping him with his powers.

After a moment, Avery turned to me, and absolute fear and guilt slammed into me. His feelings.

I faced him, forcing a mask over my face, bracing for his words. He held his hands across his stomach and he glanced away, his mouth open but no words came out.

"Avery." My words were a whisper but the room was so quiet, he could hear them. "Tell me."

He looked into my eyes, giving me a pleading look. I bit my lip, forcing myself not to react.

"Lizzy, I..." He paused and his eyes were so penetrating, so guilty, so desperate. "I'm the one who shot you in the woods."

"What!?" I froze. Tears sprung to my eyes.

"You bastard!" Easton smashed his fist against Avery's face again. Hunter moved toward me, trying to pull me in his arms but I slipped away from him just as his arms wrapped around me.

I'd shifted so quickly, so seamlessly, that it took a moment for everyone to realize that I'd done it. And that moment was all it took for me to leap out the door and run off into the woods.

8

*M*y lungs burned. My legs pounded. My heart ached.

A deer sprinted away, it's white tail showing, and other small animals rushed towards their homes. Fearing the new white wolf in the woods.

I pushed myself, hard, harder, as far as my long legs would launch through the air. Barely clinging to the mud in between steps. I almost slammed into trees, sprinting so fast that trunks enlarged in my vision the second before I veered around it. The wind whipped my hair. Smells assaulted my senses and then passed a moment later.

Voices filled my head, yet only one mattered.

I shut them all off, flinging myself into the darkness of the forest. The darkness his betrayal threw me into.

A loud crashing sound brought me to my senses and I glanced backwards.

Dragon wings veered and stumbled through the woods, breaking small trees and shredding skin.

Avery was chasing me.

No! No. I lowered my body to decrease the friction of my body, and my steps grew more agile. I pushed myself even faster. Away from him. Away from the truth.

He'd been right all along.

I didn't want to know the truth. I couldn't handle it.

I jumped over logs and boulders. I smelled a body of water and headed away from it. The open space would only give Avery the advantage he needed to catch me.

The ground was slippery, wet from the melting snow and water sprayed over my fur as I rushed through it. My feet were wet, my fur was getting muddy and cold was seeping through my bones. I stumbled, tripping over a log. I grunted as I slid across the muddy terrain and then Avery's arms wrapped around me.

Panicking, I squealed out. Wiggling my hips, I tried to slide out from his hold. Tightening his grip, he lifted me up in the air. I strained against him, pushing at his arms with my paws but his hold was too tight. I growled, angry now, showing my teeth.

"Stop it, Lizzy, just let me explain."

I shifted into my human form and he had to grapple with me to keep his hold on me.

"You tried to kill me. There's nothing to talk about." His arms were around my waist and I pushed against him. "Let me go!"

He crushed me to him, growling. "Just let me land. We're too high up." I looked down, just now noticing that we were high over the tree line. I clasped my arms around him, afraid he would drop me. He flew lower, heading for the river.

As soon as he landed, I jumped out of his arms, forcing space between us.

"Please, Lizzy, just let me explain."

"There's nothing you can say, Avery." I couldn't stop the rage in my voice, the anger that churned my stomach at the violence of his betrayal. "You shot me. That pretty much says it all." It was so cold and wet, and the wind blew through my hair, biting my exposed skin. I clasped my arms around myself, shivering. I couldn't stop shaking. He stepped closer but I backed away.

"No. Don't touch me. You don't have a right to touch me."

"I just want to warm you."

I shook my head. "I'm not cold, Avery."

"Then why—"

"I'm angry. I'm so angry, I can't stop shaking." I stared at him, trying not to cry, not to scream. I considered shifting, running away again. But I knew it wouldn't do any good. He would just chase me again. "What? Tell me whatever it is that you want to tell me. Then get the fuck out of my life."

Now my voice was the angry one, the one aimed to hurt.

He began to pace and I grew angrier by the second because he wasn't talking. He stopped and yanked off his jeans, holding them out to me. I grabbed them and jerked them on, stepping away from him.

"How could you? I trusted you! And how the fuck are you the angry one? How could you be so angry *at me*? What did I do to deserve that kind of treatment? These past few days, you acted like I was the one who shot you!"

"I know, okay! I know."

"Then why? How could you?" My voice was on the verge of breaking and that just made me more angry. I wasn't sad; I was furious.

"I was trying to push you away, okay? I didn't want you to touch me, to hold me." He looked up at me. "To look at me like I deserved any kind of love from you."

"You!" I pointed at him. "It was you. It wasn't Easton." I remembered that feeling before I had sex with Easton, right inside the house, when I'd felt despair. Such darkness. I thought it was coming from Easton, but that part. That was Avery, not Easton. "Why'd you do it?" Now my heart was breaking, now I was upset.

"I don't know how to explain."

"Well you'd better come up with something! Or I'm going back to the cabin."

He stepped forward but halted at my hard look.

"Okay, fine." He started pacing again. "Have the guys told you what I do? What my job is?"

I rolled my eyes. "Are you kidding me? And break the bro code?" I changed my voice to imitate Hunter's voice, "Avery has to tell you himself." Then I deepened it, like Easton's. "That's not for me to say."

He took in a deep breath and stopped and I suddenly realized that he hated his job. That it ate away at him. It made him hate himself. Looking me in the eyes, he took a step forward. It was tentative, asking me for permission. When I didn't stop him, he moved even closer.

"Elizabeth, I'm a sharpshooter. That's my job."

My mind whirled. "Like a sniper?"

He nodded. "Yes, but more specialized. I don't go out in the war zones anymore. They only use me for high-level operations." His eyes darkened. "And I never miss a target. Not ever."

I tried to grasp onto what he was trying to tell me. "So?"

"So? So?" His voice was incredulous, his hands fisted at his side. "You have no idea what it's like. Stalking a person that you know will be dead by the time your mission is over. I'm the angel of death, Elizabeth." He swallowed hard. "It's a hard pill to swallow. I have no idea who these people are or what they've done. I have to follow orders blindly, and it haunts me. I snuff their lives out. They will never see the people they love again."

He looked so pitiful, and yet, it wasn't enough to even let a strand of anger go.

He took another step closer. "I met Sophia that morning, do you remember? You were at Hunter's apartment and we weren't supposed to be with you?"

I nodded, remembering everything. The look on his face when he knew he would be working in the morning.

"Sophia met me the next morning, handed me a sealed file. Said I was to open it when I was alone." His hand reached for me, but I didn't move and it fell to his side. "You have no idea what it was like when I opened that file and saw your name. I was in shock. I couldn't even believe it. For a second, I thought there was a mistake, which is crazy. You don't order a hit on somebody as a *mistake*. So I knew that this was real. Someone, high up in the Authority, with access to the highest levels of the military, wanted you dead."

My heart was pounding so hard in my chest, it was making me ache. His face was a mixture of horror and shame.

"What did you do?" I couldn't stop myself from asking. I held no doubt that he could've shot me at any time. He had plenty of chances. And yet, he was gone for days. What was he doing the whole time?

He stared at the river behind me. "I tried to find out who ordered the hit. I spent days watching Sophia and Andre. Who went in and out of Andre's office. I broke into his office, went through his files, his assistant's files, Sophia's files. I followed people whom I thought could be the key to finding out. I went to their homes, and when they left, I broke inside. Went through their houses, looking for something, anything, to find the truth." He shrugged, his dark look mirroring his frustration. "But I couldn't find anything. No secret files, no plot to kill you or the Queen." My mind tumbled, assessing this new information. "Maybe there's no secret files. Just a hit. Maybe it was just Andre and he wanted you dead." He paused, thinking. "Except, that doesn't feel right. He's too smart for that; he wouldn't have assigned me to it. He'd have assigned someone else."

He began pacing again and I pressed my arms against my chest, now shivering with the knowledge of how easy it would've been to kill me. How lucky I was that Avery was the one assigned to do it. Was it mere luck that had kept me alive?

He continued. "I decided the only thing I could do was pretend to go through with my mission, to see if I could root out the person who betrayed us. So I followed you and Christian to the woods. And then I searched every inch of the area, checked every cabin and hotel and house in the vicinity. But there was no one!" His face was a twisted mask of anger and hate and it caught at me as he looked up, cutting off my thoughts and pulling my own anger out.

"So what, Avery?" I threw my hands in the air. "You decided that shooting me would root out the killer? And what happened when you did it? Did this mysterious person come out of hiding? Were they up in the trees, waiting? Did they jump out and reveal themselves, as soon as I was down?"

He frowned, his eyes throwing daggers at me. "It's not funny."

"I'm not laughing!"

"Usually someone meets you at the end of the mission. I don't usually write up reports but I give an unofficial account to someone. They're supposed to meet with you, even if the mission goes south. But this time, there was no one. Just a dead fucking phone number." He ran his hand through his hair. "I thought about watching Andre again but I was worried that someone else would be assigned to finish what I didn't do, so I watched you instead. Day and night, I didn't sleep. I was so worried." He rubbed his hand over his face and I noticed the dark lines under his eyes had grown even darker. "But no one else came. And I knew that I'd failed." He looked up at me now, a beseeching look, now that his story was over. He stepped forward one more time and we were only one step away from each other now.

I took in a deep breath, trying to focus on everything he'd said. Trying to rationalize in my mind why he thought it would've made a difference. How shooting me would root out my killer. He was so confident that he wouldn't miss, or hit the wrong vein. I remembered Christian's words, he said that Avery was good at his job. And that meant, that he thought he could play with my life, just because he thought he was good enough.

Nostrils flaring, I grit my teeth. I took that last step forward, closing the gap between us to jab in his chest. "So this whole time, you've been trying to tell me that just because you're good at your job, that because you were confident you wouldn't kill me, that that gave you permission to, what? You think that because your bullet missed my heart, that makes it okay to shoot me?" I shoved him and he stumbled back.

"No!"

"You think you can take on the world, figure everything out on your own. That because you're good at your job, it's okay to shoot me without talking to me first?" I picked up a rock and threw it at him. It hit him in the chest, harmlessly. "Because if you'd have taken a second to even think about it, you'd have known what an idiotic plan that was." I threw another one, and then another, just leaning over and throwing rocks and sticks and clumps of dirt and anything I could get

98

my hands on. "If you'd even just trusted me enough to talk to me about it, I'd have told you how stupid it was!"

His lack of response to defend himself, just like with Sophia, is what broke me out of my anger filled trance to fall to the ground. There was nothing left to say, nothing left to throw. My hands were filled with dirt and sandy mud but I grasped at it, trying to cling to something, anything.

"Lizzy, please." He came towards me again, his chest marked red where my stones hit him. His voice was desperate, needy, and filled with so much fucking self-loathing. There was nothing I could say that he hadn't already said to himself. He hated himself, and that's why he'd lashed out at me. He honestly didn't believe that he deserved any sort of love or forgiveness.

But the truth was, that even if what he had done was wrong; that I should hate him forever for even taking the chance; he could have redeemed himself if he'd only talked to me. Trusted me. We could've worked through it, together.

"Please, Lizzy, you have to forgive me." He knelt next to me. "I know I fucked up. And I don't deserve your forgiveness. And I failed at everything. I couldn't find the person who wants you dead. There was no trace. I couldn't stop myself from taking it out on you. I know I deserve your anger. But please don't hate me forever." He leaned forward, wrapping his arm around my waist and pulling me to him.

I was still angry. So mad at his lack of trust and furious at how he'd treated me since he got home, yet I couldn't deny that I still loved him. That even after everything he'd done, I still wanted him. That he was deserving of my love. That he deserved to be happy.

His eyes were staring intently at me, but now they weren't begging me for forgiveness. They were smoldering and needy. "I saw him, Lizzy. Christian. In the jacuzzi when he pushed you away. You were trying to talk to him, to show him how much you cared for him. And he stopped you. I wanted to wring his neck." His chest pressed against me and his hand skirted up my side. "I wanted that to be *me* with you. I wouldn't have pushed you away, Lizzy. I would've taken every single bit of love and attention that you would've given me." His eyes were on my lips and his hand was moving over my shoulder.

My body was responding to him, I was pressing my chest into his and my insides were on fire. But I was still angry, so angry. Not only for what he'd done, but for how he'd responded to me since he'd gotten home. He'd pushed me away and said such horrible things.

"Please, Lizzy. I can't live with myself if I don't earn your forgiveness." He gripped the back of my neck and smothered me with his mouth. I opened my mouth in shock and his tongue snaked forward, tracing the tip of mine. He pulled me down, flipping me over so that I was lying on the sandy ground.

His eyes roamed over my naked chest and his hands tugged at the button on the pants. "I was so cold, out in the snow. And you looked so warm and inviting. I was so fucking miserable and angry. And you were just so beautiful. You were so happy when you began to shift. I watched you through my scope and your smile..." He smiled, remembering. "Your smile is beautiful. It made me feel so warm inside just looking at you being happy."

He was looking into my eyes but his hand was sliding the too big pants down my thighs.

I didn't stop him, I couldn't. I was transfixed by his words, staring at the unicorn tattoo that laced his chest, of the price he'd already paid by opening himself to love.

His head lowered and his mouth skirted my throat. "But it's more than that. You are more than that. You are *my home.* You make me feel like I can be something again. Not a killer, or the person who lost his wife and baby. But like *a man* again. A man who is loved and cherished. Like I can mean something to this world again."

I was lost in his words as they wrapped around me. In the way that he was looking at me, touching me. His fingers were nimble and they were skirting up my stomach towards my breast.

"You are so sexy, so beautiful." His fingers moved over my chest, causing my nipples to perk and I bowed my back, pushing my breasts forward like an offering, egging him on. But the anger inside was still rolling, buckling, suffocating. I was a complete mess. My mind was telling me that he didn't deserve this, to touch me, not for the way that he treated me. For not trusting me enough to talk to me before he shot me. We could've worked on it together, instead of him trying to do everything on his own.

But my body was responding to his touch. It couldn't help wanting to feel his hands all over me.

He climbed over me; his erection pressed against my thigh as his eyes were boring into mine. He put his elbow over my shoulder and stretched his body over mine, moving his hand possessively around my waist.

"Please Lizzy. Say you forgive me. Say you want me, too. Tell me I can have you, even if it's just for now. For this one moment. Please, Lizzy." He traced his nose up my throat and I let out a strangled cry. At this, he closed his eyes, groaning and that noise made me loose control over myself. I wanted him so bad. So much that I was leaking between my thighs, that I wanted to slide myself over his erection and let him take me.

And yet, his confession wasn't enough. He had to change. To stop pushing me away. He had to trust me. Or I would never be enough. I put my hands against his arms. "You could've killed me."

I was still angry. What if he'd missed?

He shook his head, giving me a determined look. "No." His face was dark, his eyes demanding. "I never miss. I hit you exactly where I wanted to. Enough to look bad but not to kill." His knee pressed between my thigh, pushing my legs apart.

"But you didn't know that I was wearing the Queen's ring. That I wasn't healing. What if you shot that big vein in my leg? Or somewhere in my chest. I was a wolf when you shot me, it would've been millimeters away." I sucked in a breath, remembering. "And I stopped right before you shot me. I remember it clearly because my instincts told me that something wasn't right." Tears sparked in my eyes again but I was still so angry and turned on all at once that I was frozen in indecision. So I attacked him instead. "I could've bled out, Avery, and really died."

"There is no doubt in my mind that Christian would've ripped that ring off your finger if you'd been in any danger at all." He began to move his lips over my neck, kissing it tenderly and his beard scratched at my skin. He moved down my body, kissing and nibbling, murmuring against my skin. "But there was zero chance of that. I knew you'd stopped." He was at my entrance now, his mouth right over my pussy. He nudged it with his nose, pushing it just a tiny bit between my lips and I moaned. Damnitall to Avery for seducing me.

"You smell so fucking good right now." His tongue snaked out, touching the tip of my nub, setting my whole body on fire. "Please, Lizzy. Give me just one taste."

I grasped his arm, squeezing it, trying to keep my control. I closed my eyes as his tongue moved in between my lips, running up my cunt. His beard prickled my inner lips and the sting made me moan.

"Just one more," he murmured. "I just need. One." His tongue snaked out again. "More."

I arched my back, mewling, bringing my hips up to him as his tongue entered me again. I was dripping with need, with want, for his cock inside me. He pressed his hands into my knees, pulling my legs further apart. "You have the most beautiful pussy." He rubbed his nose over it. "It's so intoxicating. Your taste so addicting. You'll forgive me if I just make you come a little."

"No." My voice came out a mixture of desire and fury.

His hands ran up my stomach, pressing into my skin. "Please, Lizzy. Just a little. You have no idea how much I want you right now. How much I need you." His fingers flicked at my nipples, his lips kissing my hips. His breath over my skin was making me long to let him fill me up, to push himself into me and fill me with his dick. But I knew that this was everything to Avery, that he didn't give himself to anyone. That he needed my trust first or he would regret this.

And that I needed it also.

He had to trust me. To let me in. I wouldn't stand for anything else.

"No." My voice was firm now and he stilled, then looked up at me.

"No, Avery. You don't trust me."

His face contorted, his desire for me giving way to anger and shame and intense sadness.

I touched his face. "I can't... I can't let you in, until I know that you trust me enough, to give me everything first. To give me your heart."

He looked shocked. "That's what I'm trying to do! I'm giving you everything right now. You have no idea what I'm offering you. I haven't had sex since Mia, Lizzy." He gripped my hips tight. "I'm offering you everything."

He looked so crushed, so torn. So fucking broken that it destroyed me to do this. To tell him no.

But I knew it had to be done. I wrapped my legs around him, my actions a direct contradiction to my words because I was still turned on and wanting more. "I do know, Avery. I know that you want to give yourself to me. I also know that as soon as it's over, you'll want to crumble into yourself because you haven't forgiven yourself yet. Because you haven't opened your heart enough yet. You think that by offering your body to me, you're showing me that you care. That you love me." I put my hand on his chest, right over his heart. "But I want your trust, Avery. To show me that you can talk to me. Instead of pushing me away when you're angry. Instead of running off on your own, trying to save the world when we can do it better as a team. I want your body but what I need, is your heart."

His eyes stared into mine, so hurt and agonized; it was killing me to look at him. I closed my eyes, unable to take any more of his pain.

"You're right, Lizzy." He pulled my legs from around him. "I'm... I'm not being fair. You don't deserve this. And I..." I heard him swallow hard. "And I don't deserve you."

I opened my eyes. "That's not what I said, Avery." I sat up because he was standing up now, a determined look on his face. "I didn't say that."

His wings spread out from his back. He was going to leave me again.

"Avery." The anger was back. "This is exactly what I was talking about."

But it didn't matter, he just gave me this look. Filled with longing and anger and self hatred, but it was still determined. To leave.

"Avery!" I called out as he rose in the air. I was filled with fury now.

And hurt and anguish. "You can't keep doing this. You can't keep hurting me like this."

He shook his head. "I can't, Elizabeth. I just can't." Then he rose in the air, fully transforming into his beautiful dragon form.

I stood up. "Avery!" I was screaming. "Don't leave me like this. Don't leave me here." I burst into tears as he flew away, so frustrated and angry and so *hurt*. I was suddenly cold and shaking and I fell back to my knees, then lay back down on my side, allowing the rocks and the sand to dig into my skin. I pulled my knees up to my chest, drawing into myself, crying and doubting my choices.

Did I really believe that I could be enough to make them all happy?

I couldn't even keep the team together for one week.

I would never be enough. I had to let them go. Let them find their own happiness, their own families. And then they could still be a team again.

The only thought that kept me from completely falling apart in that moment was my need for revenge. I had to go home and kill Scarface. I was going to look him in the eyes as my blade went across his throat. And then I would disappear into the night.

It was better for everyone that way.

I lay there for a long time, so mad and angry and hurt and needing. And then a shadow passed over the sun, making it grow cold and the smell of the beach filled my nose as Christian's arms wrapped around me.

§

"No." I CRIED OUT AS THE FINE BLOND HAIR OF CHRISTIAN'S NAKED chest rubbed against my arms. He pulled me up, cradling me, then he stood up and began walking.

I kicked my feet. "Let me down." They'd sent Christian for a reason, to help me heal. Like Avery leaving meant nothing. But I didn't want to change my mind. I wanted to revel in the anger, to let it give me the courage to leave them. To kill the bastard who killed my parents. I didn't want to *not* be mad.

But his taut arms only tightened around me, keeping me in a cocoon of the safety he offered me. Warmth shot from his hands, filling my torso and spreading through my body. I slowly relaxed, no longer cold and shaking but I was still angry.

"Let me down." I looked into his eyes and they reflected my own stubbornness.

"Avery sent me." He said it to make me feel better but it only made me feel worse.

"I don't care."

"I tried to talk to you, to show you I was coming. It took me a while to find you."

I shrugged. "I was blocking."

His eyes darkened. "I don't want you to block me."

I studied his face, the way his eyes were so intent on me, the worry lines under his eyes as he scowled at me. "Why not?"

"Because. I just don't." We were at the river's edge and he hesitated before taking a step into the clear water.

"I thought I didn't matter to you." I spit this out, knowing it was a lie, but I wanted to get a reaction out of him. I wanted to make him just as angry as I was. Then maybe he would let me go.

"Don't play that shit with me. You know I didn't say that." Frowning, he waded in deeper and I took in a deep breath as the water touched my bare ass. I was expecting it to be freezing with the melting snow but it was the perfect temperature. His fingers dug deeper into my skin. "Don't ever block me."

"Tell me why. 'I just don't want you to' isn't good enough."

"Because I was worried about you."

"That's not a good enough reason."

He growled. "Yes it is."

"I have a right to privacy. To have some space if I need it."

We were waist deep in the water now but he kept moving down the lazy river. "Not if you're alone in the middle of the woods with a high-level target on your back, you don't. You are part of the team now, you're our fucking Alpha for hell's sake."

I sat up, forcing his arms loose, and wrapped my legs around his torso. I stared into his eyes. "Is that all I am to you?"

Pausing, he closed his eyes. "No, of course not."

"Then what, Christian?" I knew I wasn't being fair to him. Unlike Avery, he'd been clear with me. But I couldn't help taking my anger out on him. "What am I?" I was never more sure that I'd come in between them. I'd asked Christian to do something he didn't want.

It was wrong; I would never be enough for him. I understood that now.

Avery had opened my eyes, showing me that my weaknesses would only drag them down. They were too special, too important to break apart. They needed another dragon, one strong enough to handle them all.

I leaned my head against him. What was I even doing?

The water on my feet was so warm, so comfortable, and I slid down just a little bit. That's when I realized that he had an erection. It was thick and long and it was perfectly positioned under my opening. Just a little bit lower and I could slide right over it.

He looked away, biting his lip. I forced his face back to look at me.

"What are you doing? Why are we in the water?"

The emerald green of his eyes darkened and they stared into mine intently. He lifted his face stubbornly. "We're here to finish what you started in the jacuzzi."

I took in a sharp breath. "No."

He narrowed his eyes. "Why not? I want you. I want you by my side always. As my Alpha, as my friend, as my soul mate." His grip on my ass slipped just a little bit and I could feel the tip of his dick pressing into my inner thigh. "As my lover."

My expression darkened. "Don't do this just to make me feel better."

He growled. "I'm not."

"Then why?"

"Because I fucking want you, Pinky. Can't you see that?" He shifted my thighs so his thickness pressed against my stomach. "I know you can feel it."

I shook my head. "This isn't right. I can't ask you to share, to give up the intimacy you need. I'm not enough for you all."

He growled. "You are."

"I'm not!" Tears sprung from my eyes and I wiped at them, furious that I couldn't stop them from leaking down my face. "Just let me go."

He gripped me tighter, leaning his lips against mine. "I will never let you go, Pinky. Not ever."

I choked on my answer. "And the rest of the guys? I can't ask you to share with them. But I can't pick between you. I need to let you all go."

"No." His eyes were steel, staring into mine. I can..." He swallowed hard. "I can accept it."

"Can you?"

He nodded.

"I don't believe you. What changed your mind from last night?"

"It doesn't matter. Just know that I've made my decision."

I took in a breath, feeling a spark of hope. "Then I'm willing to give you the time you need, to adjust."

He growled. "No, I don't want time." He pressed his mouth against mine, snaking his tongue against my lips and fire shot to my belly. "I want you now."

I grasped the side of his face, feeling the heat between us build and staring into those stubborn eyes. The tension was still there. It had been building between us ever since that first day we met. But it had been patiently pushed back by Christian, who refused to go any further than tender kisses.

Because he didn't want to share.

Because he wanted me to himself.

What had changed?

I leaned closer, brushing my lips against his, softly, gently. He leaned into the kiss but I moved back, just ever so slightly. "You want me? You're willing to share?"

He closed his eyes, leaning his forehead against mine. "Yes."

"Then show me." I shifted my hips, causing his dick to slide in between my legs, right over my slit. The clear, warm water created a surreal atmosphere. "Show me that I am worth it."

He panted, his chest moving in and out in big breaths. "Shit, Elizabeth."

I leaned over, pressing my breasts against his bare chest. "Show me, Christian. You need to fucking show me, Christian. Because right now, I don't believe that I can be enough for you all. I don't believe that I'm worth it."

Growling, he gripped my ass, squeezing it tight. "Don't listen to Avery's lies. The only reason he's so worked up is because he feels so deeply. And you do that to him. You are everything, Elizabeth. Believe me when I tell you that." He groaned as my softness brushed against him. "Right now, I would do anything to slide my dick up inside that sweet pussy of yours. Tell me what to do, and it is done. Tell me what you want, and it's yours."

"What I want, is for you to tell me why you want it. Why now?"

"Because Pinky, you are worth it. You are my queen, and I will do anything to keep you."

"But why now?"

He opened his eyes. "Because you need it. I need it. I need to give this to you because you're hurting and I will do anything to make you feel better."

I blinked. "Because of Avery? Because he hurt me?"

He shook his head. "No. Because I love you, Pinky. Because I love you so much that it physically hurts when I see you with the other guys. But it tears me apart to think of leaving you, to imagine giving you up. Because I want to smash Avery's face for leaving you like that. Because I will give anything to take your pain away. Because when I saw you lying on the ground, so torn up and upset, I knew I would do anything to make you feel better." He rubbed his nose against mine. "Including giving you my heart."

A warmth washed over me, his words healing me more than his power ever could.

"But what about you, Christian? You need to want this."

"This is what I want." He hesitated. "Yes, I want you to myself but I see how much the whole team needs you. I want to hold you and kiss you every morning and yet, I see how happy you make them too. Even stupid Avery. And this decision is finally setting myself free. By making this decision, I can fully be with you." His lips raked over mine. "By giving this to you, I'm giving myself the greatest gift I can give myself: you."

I felt so powerful, so cherished and yet, a weight settled in my chest. I needed to be worth his love, to give him everything he ever wanted so that I would be worth what he was giving up.

I wrapped my arms around his neck and rubbed my cheek against his. "What do you want, Christian? Tell me, what do you need?"

"Right now, I need to bury myself in you. To feel you wrapped around me. For you to show me that you want me too."

I took in a deep breath. "Fuck, Christian." I leaned up and slid his cock inside me. He gripped me tighter, shuddering.

"Is this what you want? What you need?" I moved my hips, groaning and grinding and feeling and fucking. Fucking him, the man who was willing to give something away that was so precious, so guarded, and so valuable.

"Yes, Pinky. That's what I want." He was a bigger person that I was, and fuck if I didn't feel so loved and cherished that he thought me worth his love.

"You need my pussy, wrapped around your thick dick?" I wrapped my arms around his neck, kissing and nibbling. Not being gentle, but crushing my lips against his harshly. I tasted his lips, his teeth, his tongue. His chest hair rubbed against my breasts, causing a prickling sensation, and I ran my hands through the back of his head, pressing his face closer. Needing him closer, needing to feel his whole body against me. I pumped my hips, moving over his erection. "I want you, Christian. Your thick dick inside me, filling me up. You make me so fucking hot."

"You have no idea what you do to me. How I think of you before I go to bed. How your sexy fuckable body fills my mind when I shower."

"Do you jack off when you shower, Christian?"

He nodded his head, moving mine with it as our tongues tangled. "I can't help it. You make me so hard. I need it."

Suddenly a knifelike pain spread out from his hands, followed by a shot of pleasure. It moved up my back and I broke the kiss to arch my back into him, shoving him deeper into me. I took in a sharp breath and raised my eyebrows. His eyes stared into mine, deep and smoldering.

"Did you like that?"

I nodded, biting my lip.

"Do you want more?"

I shifted my hips in anticipation. "Yes."

He did it again, except this time it started out a dull throb, toying with the pulsing nerves of my body, and it gradually increased until it was shooting up my back. I moaned, throwing my head back and increasing my pace on his dick. I wanted, needed him. I closed my eyes, feeling the ecstasy as he used his power to bring me close to the edge. All I could feel was his thickness filling me up, the ebb and flow of the knife's edge of pain that was like no other. Then a sensation of utter passion washed over me, like a climax in my mind. I cried out, lost in a haze of lust and desire.

He bit my shoulder and I gripped his hair, fisting it. The slow burn of agony moved through me again, flowing through my hips and I groaned, graveling against him. "Shit, keep doing that." I moved faster, pumping my hips and kissing him. He gripped my hips, moving them, egging me faster.

"Don't stop, Christian. It feels so good." A sharpness of pain hit my clit, followed by a wave of exquisite pleasure. It wrapped around my whole body and I grasped and thrashed against him, scraping my nails down his back as my orgasm came.

I rode it out, still grinding my hips against him as his strong and muscled arms held me over him. I opened my eyes, panting and needing more, needing him to come, to have his orgasm. Christian's eyes were closed, his face filled with desire. I moved faster, driven with the need to consume him, to have his cum shoot up inside me, to know that he was so fucking in lust with me that it pushed him over the edge.

"Shit, Pinky. Don't stop. Don't stop."

I moved faster, and his arms gripped me and then his mouth dropped open as he fell over the edge.

I watched the pleasure roll over him, loving the way he looked and knowing that I did that. Knowing that he loved me, that he would share me. A pressure, warm and crushing, filled my chest as tears sprung to my eyes. He did love me enough. I could *be* enough.

I burrowed into his chest and he slipped lower into the water so that it came up to our chest. Sitting down, he rested me on his knees, and held me close.

I listened to his heart, to the air moving through his lungs, to the gentle flow of the water. The air here was clear, clean. We were in our own paradise. He ran his gentle fingers through my hair and his love for me was so intense, so warm and giving that it filled me up. I was so lost in the emotion and in the feeling, that a tear rolled down my cheek.

His chest expanded as he took in a deep breath. He cupped his hands around my cheeks, forcing me to look up into his eyes.

"I love you, Pink. You are everything to me. I will give anything to be with you. And I will learn to share."

I ran my nose over his cheek, feeling his silky skin against mine. "I will be anything, do anything you need, to make sure you don't regret it."

He shivered and studied my eyes. "Do you love me, too?"

I nodded. "Yes. I do."

He kissed my forehead, my eyebrows, my nose, and then, softly, my lips. Then he pulled me to his chest again, swallowing me up in his large body and he whispered softly. "Thank you."

I let the sound of water flowing around us whisper its secrets. "Christian? Why the water?" I looked up at him, my eyebrow raised.

He grinned and a rose blush marked his cheeks. His thumb stroked my back, shooting soft prickling sensations up it.

"What?" The way he was touching me, with the prickling and the shots of thrill. I wanted more. I needed more. "Tell me."

He shifted his face to the side but I gripped his chin. "Tell me." I kissed him, wrapping my arms around his neck. "Tell." My lips traveled down his chin to his neck and I sucked it softly, while rubbing myself against his dick. "Me."

He moaned, pressing his hand to my neck, pushing me closer. His hips twitched as his cock responded to me. Fucking dragons, I loved how fast they recovered.

I ran my fingers softly down his chest. "What is it?" I moved to his nipple and nibbled the tip. He jerked back. His stubborn eyes held mine as I looked up at him.

"Tell me." I raked my teeth over his nipple, then bit it.

He yelped, throwing me back into the water. I went under, feeling the soft touch of the water spread my hair. I came to the surface, a grin on my face. "Don't like that, do you?"

"Not after I come." He grinned as I moved my mouth towards his nipple and nudged it with my nose. "Fine." I raked my teeth softly, ever so soft over it. "But tell me anyway."

He sighed. "Okay."

He tugged at the bottom of my chin, pulling me up to kiss him softly. I climbed back into his lap and his erection pressed into my stomach.

"Because." His thumb traced my bottom lip and I bit it softly, running my teeth over it. He stared at it, not looking in my eyes. "I've wanted you ever since Hawaii and I..." His cheeks were turning a soft pink. "One of my favorite, erm..."

I raised my eyebrow. "Fantasies?"

He nodded. "Were of you in the ocean. And I knew that a hot spring emptied into this river. It would be perfect."

I wrapped my arms around his neck. "Like what, what was your favorite fantasy?"

His serious eyes were on mine now. "We were on a deserted Caribbean island."

I kissed him softly, gently. "And that totally makes sense since you are a dragon and we could fly away."

He shrugged, wrapping his arm tighter around my back.

"What else?" I kissed him again, rubbing myself against his erection. His lips closed around mine, sucking my tongue into his velvety mouth. I pulled back.

"What else?"

He groaned. "And the only clothes you had were torn and very... revealing."

"And were the other guys on the island?" I smirked, teasing him but he was suddenly harder and I grinned. I pushed over his hardness, forcing him inside me.

He groaned, dragging in a breath as I moved slowly, swirling my hips and teasing him. "You like that, Christian? Like the thought of me fucking someone else?"

He threw his head back. "Yesss."

"Ohhh." I thought about the irony of that, grinning. "But you know that I want you too, don't you Christian? That I've wanted you ever since Hawaii too, but you're the one who put me off."

He nodded. "I." He took in a breath. "Know."

I leaned in, softly rubbing my lips against his. "That fantasy sounds amazing. We should totally make that happen sometime."

He closed his eyes, giving in to my kiss as we slowly fucked again. "We totally should."

❧

I BURST THROUGH THE CABIN DOOR, SHIFTING FROM MY WOLF BACK INTO my human form. I felt the flow of magic behind me as Christian shifted back into his human form, then he followed me into the cabin. Hunter and Easton were waiting for us, having seen us coming through the video feed.

Hunter was by the monitors, a rifle in his hands. Easton was right by the door and he handed Christian his uniform. When he didn't give me anything, I gave him a pleading look; it was unlikely my uniform survived my shift. Grinning, Easton jerked his head towards my shredded uniform, which was spread out on one of the mattresses. "It's over there."

I put my hands across my chest. "You don't have any other clothes here?"

He shrugged. "Just the blankets."

"Here, Pinky." Christian began to pull off his uniform but I just grunted, disappointed, and walked towards the blankets.

Hunter sighed. "Easton, quit screwing with her."

Easton grinned but pulled Avery's shirt out from behind him and handed it to me. "I just wanted to see what she would do."

As I pulled it over my head, I remembered I'd left Avery's pants on the shore of the river. Dangit.

Hunter smirked at Easton. "You just wanted to see her naked."

He shrugged again. "Maybe."

"How about your pants, Easton?"

He leaned into me, brushing his hands over my thighs. "I think we all prefer you to be the one without anything else on."

He grinned, and no one else argued with him. He studied me silently, and I felt the bottom of Avery's shirt, making sure that it was covering all the important bits. But his eyes shifted from me, to Christian, and I gave him a small nod, answering his unspoken question. Then I took in a deep breath and began to speak.

"Okay, we're not going to wait any longer. We're leaving as soon as I fix the mask. Then we're going to confront Andre directly." I looked at Hunter. "He's requested a meeting to talk about the file we stole."

"Fine." Hunter got up and began to pack up the rifle. "We should be fine, we haven't seen anyone since we got here. Plus, Easton flew the area recently; there are no signs of anyone else coming."

So he'd probably seen us in the river.

I swallowed, looking at Easton. "And Avery?"

He shook his head. "I didn't see him."

I took in a deep breath. "Okay." I bit my lip thinking. "We'll deal with him later. Let's get ready."

The cabin was already clean and everything was packed. The trash was bagged up by the door, we'd take it with us so it didn't rot in the unused cabin.

We sat on the floor with the mask still in its case. I sat on my knees to make sure nothing showed but Christian gave me a folded blanket and I put it over my lap. Then I faced all three guys.

"First, I wanted to just clear the air."

Christian grinned and looked away. Easton and Hunter quietly waited for me to finish. They all knew what was coming.

"I've never thought that I would fall for four guys all at once, but that's exactly what's happened. I would like to take you up on your offer, to share you all, except that..." Taking in a deep breath, I pulled my shoulders up and held my hands out. "Except that I know that you all have been struggling with it a little bit. I need to make sure that everyone is happy with that decision."

"Is that what you've decided then, for sure?" Easton wanted me to be clear.

"Yes." I nodded, sure of myself. "What do you all think?"

"I'm in." Easton answered first, looking at Christian and Hunter. "I want the team to stay together and I think we work well enough together to keep things as they are. We can all share." He looked back at me. "As long as you keeps things fair and don't play favorites."

I nodded. "I agree."

Hunter looked at Christian. "You?"

Christian stared at Hunter for a moment, and Christian nodded his head.

"Are you sure, man? I know you had other plans, after everything that happened wit—" He looked at me. "That happened before."

Christian's lips grew firm and he turned to me. "This is what I want, too."

I grinned then turned to stare at Hunter. Even though he'd already given me an answer, I wanted everyone to hear it. He leaned in to give me a kiss. "Absolutely, Princess." Butterflies flit through my chest and I smiled.

"What about Avery?"

Hunter and Easton laughed.

"He'll get over it." Christian answered me.

"Are you sure?" I raised my eyebrow.

They all nodded.

"Yes, we're sure." Easton's voice was firm.

I took in a deep breath, feeling such relief and then Easton reck-lessly yanked me to him, claiming my mouth. Fire shot to my belly as his hands ran through my hair, tugging it through his fingers. A hand moved my hair to the side, then Hunter was kissing the back of my neck, his fingers brushing against my thighs to edge my shirt up higher. His hands moved up my stomach, bringing my shirt with him. His fingers softly claimed the skin right under my breasts, which were pebbled tightly at the tip, still kissing the back of my neck.

A shot of burning electricity ran up my leg and into the vee of my thighs and Christian pushed my ass forward, biting the skin right below it. His tongue roughly licked my skin, then kissed it gently. Pinpricks of pain mixed with pleasure moved up my thighs as he worked his way closer to my inner thigh.

All three men were claiming me at once, sending shots of ember and flame across my senses. I was swallowed up, drowning in emotions and of lust and power. I was a blaze of sex and fucking and sin and my necklace burned into my skin.

Easton growled, pulling my hair tight to force my head up. I opened my eyes; his were trained fiercely on my face.

"Guys." His voice was low and tight. "Guys, stop. I think she needs a break."

I looked down to see that the skin under my necklace was bubbling from the heat and blue magic was flowing through the air, surrounding us with its energy. It pressed against the sides of the cabin, threatening to burst it open.

Easton leaned back, letting me go. Christian sat up and turned my face towards him, kissing me softly. Hunter's hands moved up my sides to the top of my chest, healing the skin under my necklace. Then he moved his hands away and only Christian was kissing me. The magic softened, slowly dragging across the room towards me. His kiss was warm and soothing. Then he bit my lip playfully and dragged his lips away from mine.

I stared at them, biting my lip and blushing. "Whoops."

Taking in a deep breath, Hunter dragged his hand through his hair. "Well, then. Maybe just one-on-one from here on out."

Easton just grinned and Christian moved his hand up to my shoulder, nodding. I gave him a snarky look, knowing how he really felt.

Easton grabbed my arm and pulled me to him, wrapping his arm around me tight, and kissed me again. His lips were soft but his kiss was demanding. Then he pulled away. "Let's get this shit done. We'll find Avery soon and sit on him until he gives in."

I laughed. "Hells yeah." I looked at Hunter. "Call Liam. Tell him we're leaving in twenty."

"CHRISTIAN, CAN YOU SIT BEHIND ME PLEASE?" WE WERE ALL FACING the mask now, and I was relying on my powers to fix it. He nodded and pulled me into his lap. I leaned into him as he wrapped his arms around me. He felt so good, so comforting. I took in a deep breath, feeling a huge weight lift off my chest as I looked at the men around me.

Mine.

Grabbing Hunter's hand and, stroking it softly with my thumb, I put it to my chest. Easton put his hand on my knee. I wrapped my other hand around my mother's necklace. It was *my* necklace now, my mother's legacy. I closed my eyes, focusing on it and the magic inside awoke. It burned and pulsed in my palm.

Letting the necklace go, I moved my hand over the mask. I searched inside myself, clinging to the spark of magic, then breathed life into it.

It surged, billowing inside and around me. It spread out and clung to my guys, caressing them softly. It loved them just as I did.

I focused the magic now, moving it towards the mask. It channeled like a funnel, pouring into the mask. I opened my eyes; the magic flowed through the eyes and mouth in an eerie whoosh, moving the edges together. It also surrounded the bullet, and I knew it was fixing anything there, pulling out any malignant intent.

Then it finished, molding and sealing the mask together. The mask rose in the air, just like the book had that day that seemed so long ago. Suddenly the blue magic burst through the room, dispersing just as quickly as it came and I held my hands out, catching the mask. It looked like it had never broken.

A grin broke out on my face and Hunter leaned over to rub his mouth across my cheek, whispering in my ear. "You are so fucking sexy when you fix ancient shit with your magic."

I grinned. "Watch how sexy I get when we confront that bastard Andre."

9

I took in a deep breath, pausing outside the entrance to Andre's building. Hunter stood in front of me, taking my hand. His breath tickled my neck and I looked up.

"Everything's going to be fine."

I smiled. "I know." I swallowed hard. "I've lived my whole life with Garrett breathing down my back. Always insulting me when my dad wasn't around. I always knew that he hated me. But I knew it was because he wanted to be the Alpha. He wasn't strong enough to take down my dad, so he took it out on me." I played with his fingers. "But then I come here, and now someone else wants me dead." I looked into his eyes. "Maybe it's me. Maybe I bring out something in people. Maybe I'm just cursed."

He nuzzled my cheek. "Maybe it's because you're so strong, so inspiring, that other people are afraid of what you could do."

"What do you mean?"

"Well," he ran his hand up my neck, splaying his fingers over my jaw. "If I wanted to take out a Queen, I'd take out her strongest defender first."

I chuckled. "I think that would be Gerard."

He nuzzled my nose. "I don't think so. I think you just beat one of the toughest, bitchiest dragons in front of thousands of people." His hold tightened on my jaw, tilting my head to splay my neck. "Regardless of Gerard's skills, you'd be the one I went after."

Then he bent down and raked his teeth over my skin and I shivered. Growling, I grabbed his chin to pull him into a kiss. His taste still sweet on my lips, I turned towards the tall and imposing building, steeling myself. "Let's get this fucker."

As soon as we walked in the door, all eyes were on us. Apparently they'd all heard about the fuck-up at the museum. Used to a lot of people staring at him, Hunter stepped forward, leading us inside. The inner foyer had a natural light that filtered through the wall of windows behind us. The floor was a black marble, and stamped with the military logo in gold and silver. We walked towards a security desk that had a large black archway next to it. Orange lights shimmered under it, forming a magical alarm system of some sort.

Hunter took out his identification but the security guard didn't even look at it. His eyes were on me, instead. "Put your guns on the table, please."

Hunter, Christian and Easton all placed their guns on the table. Then Hunter and Easton walked through the arch. Christian put his hand on my back, urging me to go before him. I walked through it and an alarm went off.

The security guard stood up. "Miss, do you have any magical items?"

I nodded, and pulled out my necklace. His eyes widened as he saw it. I stared him down, challenging him to ask me to take it off. He just nodded his head. "Move forward, please."

I jumped forward, ready to be through with this. As soon as Christian was through it, I followed Hunter towards the elevators.

I stared into the mirror as we shot up to the twelfth floor and grinned. All my guys were in the exact same pose. Arms crossed, legs spread, shoulder length apart. Serious looks on their faces. They were brothers again, a team, facing their mega boss.

Making a hummph noise, I mirrored their stance, feeling more powerful. I wasn't happy about this either. I was going to kick his ass if we found out it was him. There was a bing and the elevator door opened to a reception lounge. There was no one at the front desk but it didn't matter. The guys were here often enough that they breezed on by. We moved down a long hallway, passing several other hallways filled with offices.

Suddenly, arms reached around my stomach and jerked me into a dark hallway. The smell of Avery assaulted my nose as he pressed me against the wall.

"I can't stay away from you, Lizzy."

A mixture of anger and elation ripped through my body. Avery was back! I growled. Avery was back. That motherfucker who left me alone in the woods was back.

His hands held me to the wall and he leaned against me as his voice vibrated over my ear. "I tried to fly as far away from you as possible. I went as far as the Aerwyna border but I discovered that I could fly to the edge of the earth and you will always call to me. Like a heartbeat waiting for the next, your heart will always call to mine." Avery rubbed his ear up my neck, his trembling voice sounded in my ear. "I can't breathe without you by my side. I cannot move, think, eat, smell or live without you. Tell me you fucking forgive me, tell me I can have you, and I will do anything in my power to make up for everything I've done."

I squirmed in his arms, moving to face him as Hunter, Christian and Easton rounded the corner, ready for a fight. They halted as soon as they saw Avery, but they couldn't stop their motion in time before colliding into us. Avery twisted his body to take the force of them slamming into us.

"What the hell, man?" After pulling apart from everyone, Christian grabbed Avery by the shirt. Easton and Hunter scowled, looking pissed.

I faced Avery. "Where did you come from? How did you know we were here?"

He shrugged, managing to look relaxed even though Christian had him by his shirt. "I told you, I'm very good at my job. I know how to make myself invisible." He looked at Christian, giving him a serious look. "Let me go."

Christian growled, shoving his face closer. "Not until I kick your ass for leaving Elizabeth like that, you bastard."

Avery held up his hands in a gesture of surrender. "You're right. I deserve it."

Christian growled but his hold loosened on Avery's shirt. I knew he was going to let Avery get away with it because of that pitiful look on Avery's face, so I took a step forward and punched him in the face.

"Damn straight you deserve it."

Laughter burst through the hallway and even Avery joined in.

I folded my arms across my chest, unamused. "What do you want, Avery?"

Blood dripped from his nose and it gave me a sense of satisfaction. This was probably the third time today he'd gotten his nose smashed in. Not that he didn't deserve it.

Glancing at the guys, he gave me a supplicating look. "Can we talk? Alone?"

I shook my head. "No. You can say what you have to say right here, in front of everybody. They've got my back."

Christian crossed his arms across his chest and leaned against the wall, giving Avery a stern look. Hunter and Easton nodded, smirking at him. Avery quickly looked away and at me, sighing.

"Fine." Avery took in a deep breath and put his hand on my waist, focusing on me. "You were right. About everything. I'm sorry. And I…" He rubbed his thumb across his lower lip, hesitating. "I thought I could forget about you, but I couldn't. I didn't even get very far." He sighed. "I'm weak and a coward."

"Mmm," I agreed.

He wrapped his arms around me, bringing me to him. "But I want you, Lizzy. I can't fucking live without you. Tell me, what can I do to make it up to you."

My heart was trembling in my chest, beating like mad because the part of me that had been missing, the part that longed for the four of my men together, the ache in my chest was soothed. Avery was here again.

But I stood my ground, ignoring my heart. "Tell me the truth then, Avery. What the hell has all this been about? Your screw up, I can forgive. It was dumb, but we all do dumb things. Why weren't you honest with me when you got back? Not only did you shut me out, but you were so mean and hateful. And it hurt like hell." I couldn't stop the emotion in my voice.

His lip trembled and his eyes clouded over, but he still held me close, gripping me like he was never going to let me go.

"The truth is," he swallowed hard. "The only other time I've felt this way was when Mia died. And I," he choked on his words and tears streamed down his face, "When the wolves attacked, I couldn't save her. They tore her to pieces, right in front of me. And I couldn't do anything to save her."

He took in a breath, looking away for a moment. I reached up and pulled his chin to look at me.

To look at *me*, and tell me, *to my face*.

He stared into my eyes. "And when I came back and saw you, I realized how much I fucking felt for you. I already knew I was falling for you, but seeing you and knowing what I did was too much. I was so disappointed in myself for failing you. And I worried that I would keep failing you. That someone would get to you eventually and that I wasn't able to protect the only women I've ever loved. So I thought that by pushing you away, that if I made you hate me, that..." His voice faded, breaking as he choked out the last of his words. "That it wouldn't break me in two if I failed you again."

A gut wrenching pain tugged at my throat; he was in so much pain. I let his pain, his sadness and heartbreak seep into me so that I would understand him. *This* was being an Alpha. It was being courageous enough to take their pain, to be strong enough to carry their burdens.

He leaned forward, brushing his lips against mine softly and I closed my eyes.

"Avery, I'm going to tell you the same thing that Easton told me. You have a team now. We're here to back you up. You're not alone anymore." I scowled, growling. "And we're going to fix this. Together. I promise."

He nodded and leaned his head against mine. "I know." He took in a deep breath. "I know that now. I promise, I will never do that, ever again. Tell me, what do I need to do to make it up to you? Whatever you want, I'll do. Even if I have to lick your shoes clean and do all the cooking for a year."

I raised my eyebrows. "Anything I ask?"

Nodding, his eyes burned into me. "Anything."

I shrugged. "Okay, lick my boots then."

His eyebrows went into his hair. "Okay."

"Get on your knees and grovel."

He closed his eyes and went to his knees. Easton sniggered and I bit my lips, trying not to smile.

I bent over to whisper. "Beg me for forgiveness."

He put his hands around my ankles and his lips grazed the top of my boots before I stopped him, pulling on his arm. "Stop, stop. I was just joking." The rest of the guys burst out laughing but I sighed and pulled him up.

He stood up, his sienna-burnt eyes intent on mine. "I told you, I'll do anything."

I hooked my finger in his jeans and pulled him to me. "You will do everything I say, when I say it and how I say it." I glanced at Easton who was still smirking; I guess I was learning something from him. "You will earn me, and my respect, back. Is that clear?"

He nodded. "Yes, ma'am."

I let him go and began walking again, with Hunter walking alongside me, and Christian and Easton falling in behind me. I had no idea where Andre's office was, but I was leading anyways. "Now get in line. We're going to Andre's office."

"I know." Avery jumped forward, falling in line next to Easton and Christian.

I stopped and swirled towards him, rising my eyebrow. "Excuse me?"

"I mean, yes, ma'am."

"Try to keep up." I turned back around, now unable to hold back a smile, and kept walking. We walked as a unit, with Hunter only giving me small guidance where to turn. With Avery here, everyone fell into place.

Our family was together again.

A huge weight lifted off my chest and I straightened my shoulders, focusing forward. It was time to face the man who was trying to kill me.

❧

As far as Andre knew, our appointment with him was still set up for tomorrow. We'd decided with Liam to come in unannounced to take Andre off his guard. The guys had enough clearance to get us in this far, and we weren't stopped. As we approached his office, I felt a sense of satisfaction. I had all my guys with me. We were going to kick ass.

We walked right in his office, didn't hesitate at his assistant's desk and kept moving. He jumped out of his seat, his hand on his gun strapped to his side, but when he saw us, he relaxed.

"Hey, Hunter. Guys. What's going on? Do you need to see Andre?"

We ignored him, strolling towards the hallway beyond.

"I think he's busy." The assistant, Lucian, called out to us. "You can't just go in there."

The hallway to Andre's office was lined with black tile and smooth black brick walls. I felt like we were walking the hallways to his cold, black heart. We walked in unison and the strength of my team gave me the courage to face the man I believed responsible for trying to kill me. We got to his door and I tried to open it. It was locked. I looked at Hunter.

He knelt down, eyeing the keyhole. "He's changed it. Looks like a biometric lock."

I remembered Aria's door to her garden responding to her touch. It must be the same.

"I told you, you can't just go in there. He has to open it. But I called him." Lucian's voice drifted down the hallway. "He'll be there in a sec."

"Damnit." We didn't want to give Andre any advance warning.

"Get back," I growled, ready to force it open with my magic. I closed my eyes, pulling from the magic within me. Ready to blast out in case Andre was ready with a weapon.

Suddenly, the door clicked and I opened my eyes. Andre stood there, a frown on his face. He had no weapon. He didn't look prepared for a fight. In fact, he looked bored.

"Elizabeth. Glad you could come see me." He glanced behind me. "I see you brought the Ildrenas boys, even though I requested you come alone."

I strode into the room, concealing my surprise. The guys filed in behind me then spread out. The room had been completely renovated, even the carpet was new. Light filtered from the wall of windows that looked out beyond into the city. I strode towards his desk and collapsed into the black leather sofa across from it. Hunter sat next to me and leaned back, putting his arms behind his head to relax comfortably into the sofa.

He looked confident and laid back but I could feel the tension coming from him.

Avery and Easton stood behind me but Christian skirted into the room, giving Andre a wide berth and then hung back. Instead of going any deeper in the room, he stood by the door. Andre watched him for a moment then, deliberately turning his back, and walked over to his desk. He sat down heavily into his chair and swiveled towards his desktop, which held neat stacks of paper, along with a sleek black laptop.

He closed the laptop and then, placing the palm of his hands on the top of his desk, looked up at me.

"Now. I've requested this meeting with you because—"

"What is this?" Christian was now standing by the only thing that hadn't been replaced in the room, his shelves. He picked up a gold statue and showed it to Andre. It was an elephant with several arms and looked like they were in different positions.

Andre frowned. "That is an old and priceless statue from the Indian region, known to be from an ancient Hindu temple. Please put it back."

Christian shrugged, then gently put it back and moved on to the next item, which looked like a paperweight. Andre stared at him, a scowl on his face.

Hunter sat forward. "I like your new desk. Mahogany?"

Andre's eyes didn't leave Christian. "Yes."

Hunter smirked. "Your old one, it was… ebony, right?"

Andre's eyes slid towards Hunter, his nostrils flaring. "As I'm sure you well remember."

"When did you change your lock?" Avery leaned forward, his hands on the back of the couch. The seriousness in his voice made me shiver and Andre's eyes moved from Avery to me.

I gave him a hard look and leaned forward. "Did you try to kill me?"

He looked from Hunter to Avery to me, ignoring the bump from Christian at the back, who was flipping through a book.

He looked at Hunter. "I changed my whole room the day after you two defiled it and," his eyes slid to Avery, "I changed the lock after someone broke in. Apparently, I've trained my men too well."

Easton broke in. "Charles trained us."

Andre gave him a cool look. "And I trained Charles."

Silence came over the room, except for Christian who kept flipping the pages of the book.

"Now," Andre folded his hands on the desk. "I know one of you took my file on William Erikson. That is a severe breach of protocol and I could have you arrested."

"I notice you didn't answer my question." My voice was low and my necklace warmed at my throat, just waiting to be used.

He was calm. Too calm for my liking. Was a cold-blooded killer staring back at me? The thought made my wolf come alive and the hair on the back of my neck stood on end.

He looked at Avery, avoiding my stare. "The first time I was aware of your mission was when I saw Elizabeth walk out into the arena for her challenge against Sophia." Now his eyes met mine and they were cold but intense. "I assure you, I made no such attempt against your life. In fact, the fiasco of your mission has been hell to clean up." The only thing in his voice that indicated he was feeling any kind of anger at all was a slightly frustrated lilt at the end of his sentence.

I ignored his frustration. "How did you know that Avery was assigned to kill me?"

"I would recognize his handiwork anywhere, as I've seen it several times. Except I was surprised that you were still alive. But it made sense. Big enough to look like he'd made an attempt, but in the exact spot that would do the least amount of damage. Especially for a shifter wolf like you. It was a brilliant strategy on his part."

I grunted, annoyed that Andre was giving Avery's rationalization weight. I outright ignored the fact that the only time I was seeing Andre get excited about anything, was when he was strategizing killing me.

He continued, "I immediately left the arena to look into the breach. You guys aren't the only ones that have breached my offices and I've made certain that nothing like that will ever happen again."

Avery leaned into the couch, ready to spring over it. "You expect us to believe you?"

Andre laughed. It was an eerie, brittle thing and it chilled me to my bones. "Why on earth would I assign *you* to kill Elizabeth?" He gestured towards me. "If I'd have wanted her dead, I would most certainly have chosen someone else, even if he wasn't the best. Because even you have your limits, Avery."

He looked at me, his eyes dark and serious. "And believe me, if I'd have ordered the hit, she'd be dead by now."

His words alone were harmless enough, but the way he said it, the tone of his voice, it sounded threatening. The hair on the back of my neck stood on end and a warning snarl escaped my mouth, unbidden.

A shot of blue magic shot out from my necklace into the room. Easton growled and launched himself over the couch. Hunter and Avery were right behind him. I jumped up, torn between holding my guys back and launching at him myself.

But Andre was fast. He blocked Easton's hit, then threw him across the room. Both Hunter and Avery fell in right behind Easton, tackling Andre to the ground. Avery grabbed Andre's shoulders but Andre smashed a powerful fist across Avery's nose. Avery's face snapped backwards, forcing him to fall onto his back.

Hunter straddled Andre and, bunching his hands into Andre's shirt, he leaned into his face. "Apologize right now or I will kill you before you take your second breath."

"Hunter." I tried to warn him.

Andre's hands were clutching at Hunter's stomach and in half a second, they'd turned into claws. It would only take one swipe for him to take out Hunter's guts.

Reacting quickly, I pushed my magic into Andre. It landed on his chest and I directed it towards his hands. Blue energy surrounded them, making it impossible for him to hurt Hunter.

Hunter growled, leaning so close their noses touched. "I said apologize."

Andre growled in response.

Easton was back on his feet, racing towards us. Avery was crouched next to Hunter and Andre, ready to help Hunter or Easton.

I looked up at Christian and he gave me a nod.

"Hunter, stop."

He didn't move. I wasn't even sure he heard me, he was so focused on Andre.

I felt Andre's power flowing through the room, pushing against my magic. He was trying to siphon it off. I grabbed Hunter's shirt and yanked him up. He struggled against me but I gripped him tighter and tugged with all my strength.

"Hunter, stop." I used my Alpha voice, forcing it to cut through Hunter's thoughts. "It's okay."

Suddenly, Hunter's eyes snapped to me. He relaxed, leaning against

my side, panting. Andre pushed Avery away, his claws already trans-
formed back into human hands. I pulled my power back and it
dispelled through the room.

Andre stood up and straightened his uniform, a scowl on his face,
but the tension in the room melted away. Easton held his hand out to
Avery, yanking him to his feet.

I met Hunter's eyes. "Let's go."

Hunter nodded. I let him go and, pretending to look at my wrist,
which didn't have a watch. "Well, look at the time. I think it's time we
leave, don't you?"

Andre gave me a death glare. "I'm not done with this meeting."

"Whoops. We forgot about something we have to do. I'm sorry,
we'll come back later." I met his eyes. "I promise."

A promise to kill him, if we found out he was a traitor.

Christian was already out the door, with Avery and Easton on his
heels. Hunter pulled at my hand.

Andre began to walk towards me. "Elizabeth. Don't think this is
over. You may feel safe with these men at your back but you're not."

I stopped. "Is that a threat?"

He rolled his eyes. "Of course not. But if I didn't order the hit on
you, who did? Whoever it is, is still out there. I would watch my back
if I were you."

I clutched my hands at my side. "That actually looks like something you should be doing, don't you think? Being the protector of the
Queen's assets, right?"

His mouth dropped open, the only time I ever saw him stumble.
He probably never saw himself as my protector.

He snapped it shut. "Of course. I am here to serve the Queen, as
well as you. I'm looking into it as well."

"You'd better." My voice practically came out a snarl.

His eyes were fixed on me. "You'd better watch your tone with me.
You are under the Queen's protection but I am to be respected."

Now it was Hunter trying to get me to calm down. He tugged at
my arm but I didn't budge.

"I'll show you respect once you earn it. And don't believe for a second that I've forgotten how you treated Emma and buried the news about the wolves' ability to save your little reproduction problem. Or the fact that her husband has gone missing."

He sighed and, brushing off his coat, went back to his desk. "That's not your concern."

"Are you ever going to let them go? Let them lead a normal life?"

"The Queen has been attending to them and their problems." He glanced at the clock over his door. "In fact, I think she is there right now."

I huffed, then turned away, allowing Hunter to tug me out of the office and down the hallway. "That's right. So you'd better watch *your* back! In case the Queen feels like chopping off heads."

Hunter burst into laugher and I doubted that Andre heard me but I didn't care. We'd gotten what we came for.

༄

WE WALKED DOWN THE HALLWAY, PASSING LUCIAN'S DESK WITHOUT A word. He scrambled to his feet, brushing his blond hair out of his face. "Hunter, wait."

I paused. There was something inside me, some instinct, telling me that we should listen to him. Hunter's eyes told me he felt the same thing. He stopped and broke away from the group.

Easton took my arm, pulling me forward and I stepped in line next to him and Christian. Christian looked at me, his eyes knowing, and grinned. He reached inside his pocket and pulled out a brass and silver astrolabe, an ancient artifact used to measure the stars. It was beautiful. It was also the second artifact we were tasked to retrieve, and it glowed a soft yellow. He handed it over and I slipped it in my bra.

Then we all walked together, down the hallway and towards the elevators. We passed office doors with sleek black desks, busy with important men staring at their computers and growling male assistants.

As soon as we reached the elevator, we stopped and waited for

Hunter. He caught up with us, saying nothing, so we all entered and exited the elevator without a word. The same security guard glanced at the lump of my necklace through my shirt. When he saw us looking at him, his eyes slid away towards the screen in front of him.

My necklace, and the astrolabe, set off the alarm again but the security guard just waved us through.

As soon as we were outside, Hunter took my hand and led me towards the Range Rover. When we reached the car, Avery moved ahead of us to open the passenger door for me.

I stared at him as I slid into my seat. As soon as I was in the seat, he leaned over and, for a moment we were alone. His cupped my cheeks, pulling me towards him. "I swear I will do anything to keep my promise."

Then he kissed me. Softly, gently, and I let his tender lips seal mine in that promise. When he pulled away, I gave him a warning. "You'd better."

He smiled, nodding, then he shut my door. I smiled, warmed by his touch. The other doors opened and the rest of my guys fell into the seats.

No one spoke until we were out of the parking lot. Easton spoke first. "Well that was interesting. Anybody hungry?"

Christian answered. "What about that gyro place near your apartment, Hunter?"

"Hells yeah." Avery's favorite, apparently.

Hunter turned right, entering the lunch traffic. I looked at him. "What did Lucian say?"

"He said that Andre's been working on a secret project for months. He's been staying late and acting weird."

"And that's not normal?"

Easton laughed. "Yeah, that could be a normal day for him."

Hunter frowned. "If it was normal, why did his assistant bring it up?"

I nodded. "True."

Hunter took in a deep breath. "I don't think he did it."

I swiveled in my seat to look at everyone, gaging their reaction.

"I think he's a bastard." Easton looked out the window, watching the buildings as they flew by.

"Agreed. But that doesn't mean he tried to kill Lizzy." Christian looked at Easton.

"That also doesn't mean that he didn't." Avery shuffled in his seat, getting comfortable.

Hunter interrupted them again. "There's two things we have to consider. We can't forget the main reason why we went there. Has he been taking the artifacts? And did he try to kill Lizzy? They could be separate."

I nodded and he glanced at me. "What do you think?"

I paused, mulled over our conversation with Andre, trying to decide if he was telling the truth. My instincts were telling me that he was. "I think that he could kill me just as soon as look at me. He holds no tenderness towards me. So, if he really did want me dead, he'd have done it by now." A shiver ran down my back. It gave me the creeps just thinking about it. "And I can't argue against his reasoning. He's too smart to give the assignment to Avery." I winked at Avery and he grinned. "If only for the fact that it's very possible he would've succeeded by now. It makes me sick to think about it, but it's probably true. And he's too slick to bring in a tank to the museum. That was a mess for them to clean up. For *him* to clean up."

Hunter shifted lanes; we were approaching the block with his apartment. The disposable phone rang and we all turned towards it. Hunter pulled it out of his pocket to answer. The guys continued talking, each voicing their opinions that pretty much lined up with mine. I turned forward again. There was something bugging me, but I couldn't quite figure out what it was.

Out of the corner of my mind I heard Hunter on the phone. He mostly listened, giving only affirmative answers before thanking them and hanging up.

"That was Sophia. She said that Andre was with her all night last night. He didn't seem to be anxious about anything. She also said that

Andre recently scanned the SEPN, our work internet, and found a virus. He's contained it but they're going through it now to determine what it did. She's going to his house tomorrow evening to look for any of the artifacts; he'll be in meetings late all day."

Easton spoke up. "If there was a virus, it could have started the paperwork for your mission, Avery. Sophia's assistant would have prepared it without even looking at it. They have eighty to a hundred or so missions a day."

"So I think we're pretty much agreed that it's a possibility that it's someone else at least," Christian said.

Everyone nodded in agreement and the SUV grew silent as everyone considered this.

Andre knew about my conversation with the Queen but he didn't know what she'd asked me to do unless he'd bugged her room. I closed my eyes, going back to my conversation with the Queen. We'd gone over everything she needed, including the locations for the artifacts. If her rooms were bugged, he'd have known everything. If he'd wanted the mask, he would have left immediately for it, instead of showing up with a freaking military. And why didn't he hide his own? It was just out there on his shelves, for anyone with the balls enough to take it. No, it didn't make sense. Just like him assigning Avery to kill me. It couldn't be him.

So who knew that we were going for the artifact, but not the location of it?

We turned the corner, passing right by Hunter's apartment and it made me think of the first time someone tried to shoot me. It seemed random that time, someone who appeared to be a fanatic, a wolf hater. But then the attempts on my life only got more persistent, so I didn't believe that was a random event. Someone wanted me dead from the minute I stepped into Aerwyna.

But who even knew that I was here? Sophia, Andre, the soldiers who brought me here. The Queen. And probably her two closest confidents, and my dad's friends: Liam and Ember.

My mouth dropped open, in shock for a moment.

Could it be one of them?

Liam knew I had a mission but not exactly where. Virus or not, whoever was trying to kill me had access to the snipers, but didn't know exactly which one would be chosen. They also had access to soldiers, who showed up ready to kill. But they didn't show up until after we'd been there for a while. So they were ready but didn't know where to go until after we were already there. Was it Liam?

"Elizabeth?" Hunter's voice was soft but it broke through my thoughts. I looked up. The gyro place was right ahead, just one block away. Suddenly a black SUV broke through the intersection, ramming straight into us.

"Shit." Hunter pulled back and then moved around it, running over the median and into oncoming traffic. A white truck blared its horn at us and we turned into the next intersection. Flying down the road, I looked in the side mirror. Two black SUVs were threading through traffic towards us.

The next light was red and I gripped the console, in shock. I glanced at the rest of the guys. Easton and Avery were leaning over the back seat, digging through the bags. Everyone was okay. The front of the SUV had taken a hit, but it was still running fine. Our tires squealed as Hunter turned right, going the wrong direction down a one-way street.

Clinging to the door handle, I squeezed my eyes shut until I felt a tap on my shoulder. I glanced back, Christian was holding out a bullet-proof vest. "Put this on."

The guys were prepared, I had to give them that. Trying to keep my balance in the swerving car, I pulled it over my head, noting that Avery and Easton were putting on theirs. My hands were sweaty and the Velcro slipped as I tried to strap it. Then Christian was holding out a gun and a knife.

I looked into his eyes. The gun, great. But the knife? That was for close contact. Taking them, I swallowed hard and felt my wolf alive.

"Like this." Christian showed me to tuck the knife under the bottom part of my bullet proof vest and I discovered a slit in it just for that purpose. My heart thudded as I slid it up, my sweaty palm making it slippery. I was grateful Easton had worked with me on them.

We careened around another corner into a back alley. Hunter pushed the SUV as hard as possible, shooting us down the road. We had a clear break but the black SUVs weren't far behind us.

"Help him." Christian gave me another vest, nodding at Hunter. Unbuckling my seat belt, I leaned over the console and slipped it over his head, then strapped it. His glance thanked me and I settled back into my seat.

A black SUV pulled up to my window. Their window rolled down and a man dressed in the same uniform as the men from the museum leaned out. Easton rolled down the window, just a slit. He pointed his gun, aiming for the man.

A freaking harpoon sailed out of their car. Easton shot his gun and the loud bang echoed through my ears. The harpoon landed in Easton's window, then suddenly the car beside us slowed down and our bulletproof window was yanked out.

I yelped as Hunter swerved, trying to keep control over the car. There was a loud bang, and a rocket launched towards the open window. Straightening, Hunter turned down an empty road and the rocket skimmed the side of the car and then crashed into a building. He slammed his foot on the gas and we flew down the road, air whipping through the car.

"Did you hit him?" I turned around, the two SUVs still followed us. Easton nodded. "I think so."

Shit, shit. What was that?

I tried to think of what I could do. We were headed towards the lake. If we could make it there, we'd have more of a chance. It was outside the city. Less traffic, less people.

Another SUV came barreling down the road in front of us, headed straight for our SUV. Suddenly, it turned, sliding it's back end forward so that it was blocking the road.

Hunter slammed on the brakes. We were trapped from both ends. The guys sprung into action, pulling out the rifles.

"Get ready, Lizzy." Easton warned me before he shot, and it popped loudly in my ears. Avery was next to shoot. They returned fire and the bullets ricocheted off our bulletproof car.

Christian handed Hunter a rifle, then looked at me. "Trade places with me."

Nodding, I pulled off my seatbelt and climbed in between Avery and Easton. After climbing into my place, both him and Hunter shot at the car in front of us.

Everything was so loud. The ringing in my ears got louder. I pressed my magic out, blocking the noise. I had my gun in my hand, but instead of shooting, I took in my surroundings. We couldn't stay here long. We were blocked in on both sides by tall buildings. We were like sitting ducks. I was certain that we were outmanned and outgunned. Maybe I could use my magic to blast one of the SUVs out of the way.

I scanned the buildings. The building on our left had a back door.

"Lean forward!" I yelled to Avery. "We're going through that door on our left." I pushed him out of the way, then rolled down the window, aiming my gun. I was going to shoot it open.

Then, I hesitated.

What if someone was behind it? I couldn't kill an innocent person. I was a good shot, but I wasn't going to bet someone's life on it.

There was a loud boom and I jerked back in my seat. Another one of those large rocket looking thingees was headed straight for us. Hunter and Christian opened their doors. Avery grabbed my hand, pulling me out, just as it landed. The car shook as it crashed through the front window, landing on the dash. A yellow gas spewed out of it.

"Hold your breath!"

I tried to hold it, but it was too late. I'd already breathed it in. The world immediately grew dim. Avery shoved me out in front of him and I fell to the ground. I tried to get up but my head was too heavy. Avery was halfway hanging out the car and I reached for him, trying to pull him to me.

Footsteps pounded on the ground.

Shit. They were so freaking loud.

Hunter was already passed out, lying on the ground.

Boots surrounded me.

"Search for the artifact. Only grab the girl. We can get anything we need from her." A woman's voice. The wall of combat boots separated and a pair of black heels came through, stepping over Hunter and coming straight towards me. She stopped and I looked up, blinking and trying to keep my eyes open. They were so heavy.

A halo of light highlighted her face.

"Ember." I sounded funny, my word slurred.

She smirked. "Hello, Elizabeth." She leaned over and yanked my necklace from my neck. "Don't want you using your power, do we?"

Then everything was black.

❧

I AWOKE TO A STIFLING HEAT. MY EYES WERE HEAVY AND I TRIED TO open them but I couldn't. Something scraped across the floor, and my skin felt a prickling sensation run across it. Sweat trickled down my body. It was so friggin' hot.

"Wakey wakey, little bitch."

I moaned, my eyes still not opening. I opened my mouth, but it took a minute for my brain to obey my command to answer. "I don't..." I swallowed, forcing moisture down my dry throat. "I don't think I'm the bitch in this situation."

Ember laughed, running something sharp up my thigh. "I'd have to disagree on that point."

My eyes jerked open. She was leaning over me, a knife in her hand. I eyed it warily but she took a step back and, tucking the knife in the back of her pants, she sat down.

"Thanks for the astrolabe. I wasn't sure how I was going to get it past Andre. Though, I have to admit that wasn't a very creative place to hide it, in your bra."

I smirked. "Did you cop a good feel in while you were at it?"

The side of her lips twisted up. "Maybe."

Rolling my eyes, I forced myself to sit up. What the hell was I laying on? It was friggin' hard. We were in a dark, stone room with the only light coming from a fire hearth. It glowed eerily against the stone walls.

I looked down; she'd put me on a table.

"What, couldn't splurge on a bed?"

Her grin was predatory. "Why on earth would I need a bed? I'm not planning on keeping you around for much longer."

I stared at her, studying the woman who'd been trying to kill me since I'd gotten here. The woman who'd betrayed not only the Queen, but her best friend. My eyes drifted to her black onyx ring. The one that matched mine. Given as a token of *trust.*

"I see jewelry doesn't mean much to you."

"This one does." Her hand went to her chest and she pulled out *my* necklace.

I growled. "That's mine."

She smirked. "You won't be needing it any longer. It will add nicely to the other things I've collected."

Gah, she was such a cliché. I laughed. "You won't even be able to figure out how to use it. It took me forever."

She rolled her eyes. "I'm sure it won't be a problem."

I smirked. "I doubt that."

"Unlike you, I've been trained in magical objects since I was a child. I always told Robert he should've trained you better." She shrugged. "No matter. His laziness only benefited me in the end."

I growled, the fur on the back of my neck stood on end. Fuck this shit. I wasn't going to stick around to figure out what the hell she wanted. I was going to turn into the white wolf, eat her face off, take my necklace back, and get the hell out of here.

I moved my magic over my body, ready to shift. It burst from me and then fizzled into a slow burn. I frowned and closed my eyes, focusing on the pulse of shifter magic inside. It was weak and sluggish. I connected with it, encouraging it to blossom but it only gave me a shaky response, then stifled.

I opened my eyes. "What the hell did you do to my shifter power?" I was angry now. Had she taken it from me? First, the only thing I had of my mother's, and now she'd fucked with my shifter power.

I was done with this. I didn't need my powers to kick ass.

I stood up and slammed my fist into her face. Then followed up with an upper left cut. I kicked her chair, toppling it backwards.

She fell back, yelping in pain and surprise, and the chair clamored to the floor. I jumped on top of her, grabbing for my necklace but her hand clamped down on my arm. I growled, trying to yank it out, but she held me like a vice. I punched her stomach with my left hand and she sucked in a breath. The hand on my arm grew hot; her hand was burning into my skin.

I cried out, trying to yank my arm away again, but she gripped it tighter, clamping her teeth together.

"Don't fucking hit me." She yanked my hand from her chest, pushing me to the floor and climbed on top of me, finally releasing her hand on my arm. I cradled it. Shit, it hurt like hell. Where was Hunter when I needed him? I grit my teeth, fighting against the pain.

"What did you do with my team? Where are they?"

"You think they're going to save you? Come rushing in to save the woman they love?" She smirked. "I wouldn't hold out hope for that, seeing as I ordered my men to kill them."

I gasped. "No."

"Yep." She climbed off me and grabbed her chair, putting it back on its feet.

"I don't believe you." We were connected. "I would feel it if they were dead."

"Even if they managed to defeat my team, which is unlikely considering they were unconscious when I left them, they'd never be able to find you here. We're under the castle, one room in hundreds, hidden by all the twisty tunnels and secret places that not even the Queen knows about. No one will find us here. Only Liam knows these tunnels as well as I do. And he certainly isn't looking for you." She grabbed my shirt and, hauling me on my feet, she threw me in the chair. "But no matter, they're dead. Just like you will be in a few minutes."

I searched my feelings, digging deep inside, calling out to them. But I felt nothing. No power. No connection to my guys. Nothing but this stifling heat and the pain shooting through my arm.

She sneered. "Don't feel anything, do you?"

I frowned. "It's probably just a stupid magic trick or something." I rubbed my face. "Just tell me what the hell you want."

She stepped back, rubbing her cheek where I'd clocked her. "Fine. Since you don't want to prolong your death, let's get a move on. I need to know where you've hidden the book and the ring."

"Unfortunately, I don't feel like telling you that." I jumped up and ran for the door. She didn't even move, which gave me a really bad feeling. I reached it in three steps and yanked at the handle. It didn't budge. I yanked harder, then kicked at it.

"Ugh!" I tried again, hitting and kicking the thick wooden door.

"You'll never get out. And even if you could, I have ten men outside the door, ready to kill you if you try to leave." She walked toward me. "You can't escape. You don't have any more powers. Your men are dead. No one knows where you are. No one is even looking for you." She brushed her fingers across my cheek and down my neck, gripping my shirt. "Just tell me, little puppy. Tell me where you've hidden the book and the ring and I'll make sure that you have one last night of fun before you go."

I faced her; her eyes stared into mine.

"Is that why you choose me, instead of one of my guys? Do you have a little *crush*?"

She frowned. "No."

I folded my arms. "Then, why?"

"You'll find out. After you tell me where they are." She leaned in, raising her eyebrows and pulling my arms away from my chest. Then she gripped my waist. "How about it?"

"What about Liam?"

She glanced away. "You out of all people should know that you can lust after more than one person. I'm sure you've fucked every single one of those guys."

I jutted out my chin stubbornly. "I haven't."

She huffed out a breath. "I don't know why not. Sexy men like that, all in one clan? I'd have taken them all in one night."

I looked away. I didn't like her talking about them like that. They weren't sexual objects. They were mine. Strong and loyal, loving and kind. And they *weren't* dead.

Her hand moved towards my breast but I slapped it away. "No."

She growled, and her dragon energy swelled. "I have powers you aren't aware of. I can make these last few minutes of your pitiful life the best, most erotic time of your life." She frowned, getting closer. "Or they can be your worst nightmare. You choose."

I looked into her eyes. "Just tell me one thing."

She raised her eyebrow. "What?"

"Tell me why. Explain to me how a woman like you, with a Queen at your side, a good man... Why would you betray the woman who trusts you so much?"

She huffed. "You have no idea what my life is like."

"I know you're loved. I can tell by the way they talk about you."

"And what they don't talk about are all the sacrifices I've given. For Liam. For Aria. For a people that hold so much spite." Her voice was bitter, and hate swirled in her eyes. "From my birth, they hated me. They rejected me because I'm not one of them."

"What? A dragon?" My eyes scoured the walls, looking for a way out. Maybe there was another door, a hidden one.

She sneered. "No, a pureblood."

"If they hated you so much, then how did you even know the Queen?"

"My parents were the personal attendants of Aria's parents. They served her parents day and night, waited on them hand and foot. And it didn't matter if I was sick or hurt. The majesties always came first."

I shrugged, trying not to make it obvious that I was studying every brick at the fireplace. The movies always had a hidden door behind the fireplace, right? "Seems like a worthy cause to me."

She growled, her voice growing darker, more harsh. "Hardly. Except, even I thought so once. I lived that lie a long time; I grew up with Aria. And I worshipped her. I kissed the ground she walked on.

Played with her in that stupid garden." She erupted in frustration. "I gave her everything! I did anything she asked of me. I stole cookies from the kitchen, distracted her parents so she could make out with Harry from her chemistry class. And after her parents' plane crashed, I held her while she cried. Ugh, what a weak little thing."

Shocked, I stopped my examination of the room to look into her eyes. They were cold and hard. There was no emotion in them except a hard bitterness.

"And yet, she still asks for more. She would have me give my very life for her. "

I swallowed hard. "That's what people do for the ones they love." It's what my dad and mom did for me.

She grinned, blinking, and suddenly the hate in her eyes was gone, replaced with something playful. Something sensual. It was like she flipped a switch.

She pulled on my shirt again, dragging me to her. "And you? Are you willing to give your life for her?"

"Are you giving me a choice?"

Her eyes moved to my lips. "Maybe."

"Why go after me? What am I to you? You wanted me dead before I even met you."

She licked her lips and gripped me, digging her palm into my side to push me softly against the door. "Because of the prophecy, of course."

"What prophecy?"

Her fingers ran over the skin under my shirt and a slow, sensuous feeling began to flow through my body. "About the wolf who unites the dragons with no Alpha. Who sacrifices everything to save the Queen." She grinned, and the sensual feeling grew stronger, pulsating between my thighs. I moaned.

"We have lots of prophecies, they were spoken long ago. I like to keep up with them." She leaned in, so close her breath tickled my face. "I thought it was about Emma at first. I manipulated that situation to get her out of the Kingdom. But as soon as I heard about you, I knew it wasn't Emma at all."

"But you still haven't told me why." Tired of fighting against her magic, I leaned into her, brushing my lips against hers. Her breath caught and she traced her fingers across my stomach.

"Why go through all this? Instead of being loyal to those who love you, even if they ask you to sacrifice yourself."

"Let's just say I have a gift for knowing when to cut my losses. There are beings out there, much more powerful than you or me, with powers stronger than anything I've ever seen. And one day, they will rule every supernatural creature."

Wrapping her arm around my back, she yanked me closer, pressing her lips on mine. Her hand moved inside my shirt to cup my breast and an arousing heat moved through my body, shooting to my core and I sucked in a breath.

Fuck, she did have erotic powers. Powerful ones.

She deepened the kiss, and a fervid heat tore through me where her hand was caressing my breast. Every single touch of her skin against mine sent shooting waves of desire and need up my body. "Now." She pulled back, panting as she pinched the tips of my breast. "Tell me where they are."

"I don't think so."

She twisted my nipple, sending a shooting pain through my chest that made me cry out. "I think you want this more than you realize." She gripped my chin, forcing her lips over mine again. Her hand moved down my stomach. Flames of desire licked my skin and I arched my back against the door. She released her hold over my lips and leaned over, pulling my shirt and bra up to nibble at the tips of my breasts.

"No." I pushed against her shoulders but she ignored me. Her other hand skimmed down into my underwear. She slowly caressed and touched, sending me into a frenzy of desire. Then her finger dipped inside my pussy and I couldn't control myself. I rubbed myself against her hand, needing to come.

Shit. My feelings were all over the place. I wanted to fuck her. On the floor, on the table, against the door. I also wanted to kill her. To rip open her chest and yank her heart out. I clasped her to me, torn between my desires as her lips moved lower.

"Lizzy. Tell me where they are."

I shook my head, pressing hers against my stomach.

"Yes." She bit my hip and a shot of pain rode up my body. Then she yanked my pants down and her tongue touched the tip of my vulva. I breathed heavily. Fuck, I wanted this so bad. What the hell was wrong with me? She'd tried to kill me. She ordered my men killed. She betrayed everyone and was working with the men who'd killed my dad.

But I still wanted her. I wanted to fuck her with every fiber of my being.

I had to get control over my body. I had to use her power against her.

She swiped her tongue in between my lips and I moaned, rubbing my crotch against her face, trying to draw her tongue further inside. And then I froze as a wave of shame crashed over me, revolted with what I'd just done.

She chuckled, kissing my sex tenderly, then moved her lips back up my body, pulling my pants back up. "Do you like how that feels, Elizabeth? I can give you more. I can make you come, over and over. All night, if you want. You can have one simple night in pure pleasure, before I kill you with my knife. I'll even kill you quickly, make it painless."

I wanted to crawl into myself, to throw her off me. How dare she use sex to manipulate and control me. How dare she threaten me. How dare she threaten everyone I loved.

Her lips caressed my body, which now threatened to withdraw in horror, but she didn't realize it. She was caught up in her own powers, filled with desire and lust. "We can spend all night like this, and I won't even ask for anything in return. I won't ask you to eat me out. Unless you want to." She looked up at me, grinning, and I forced my face into a mask. Her hands were on my breasts again, flicking the nubs and they perked, betraying me. Then her mouth was over them, her tongue flicking and vibrating and her powers began to move through me again. I moaned, struggling to control myself, to control my freaking libido.

I've never wanted to *not* be horny as much as I wanted it now.

Her hands moved back down my stomach, settling on my hips as her lips moved up my chest. Then she was slowly pulling down my bra and fixing my shirt. "Now, Elizabeth. You see what I can do to do. What kind of pleasure I can give you." Her face hardened. "But first, I need the information. When I've been notified that the book and the ring are where you say they are, we can begin. Just tell me where they are and I'll give you every fantasy you've ever desired. This was just a small bite, a taste, I have so much more to offer you."

I gripped her face, kissing her harshly and she leaned into me, grinning.

"My greatest fantasy," I moved my lips over her cheek, kissing her roughly, to her ear. "Is to be back with my team." I bit her ear. She jumped back and I rammed my elbow into the side of her face.

Growling, she gripped my neck with both hands, squeezing tight. Her hands were burning hot into my soft flesh, scorching through my delicate skin. Crying out, I clasped at her hand, hooking my fingers over her thumb. I yanked it down, breaking her thumb and she howled out in pain. Then she grabbed my arms and threw me across the room. I flew through the air and crashed into the table.

Suddenly the whole room was hotter, and the flame at the fireplace grew into a bonfire, throwing sparks across the room. The air pressed against my skin, making me feel groggy and weak. I clasped at the floor, trying to get up.

"Don't want to play nice, Lizzy? I was hoping for a little bit of fun. I don't mind giving you pleasure. In fact, I like doing it in exchange for something I want. I've been doing it to Liam and Andre for years. But I don't mind giving out a little pain either." She grabbed me by my hair and threw me across the room again. I crashed against the wall, landing on my knees. Pain shot up my thighs but I scrambled towards the door.

"Help!" I pounded on it, hoping one of the soldiers would feel bad for me. Hoping one of them had a sliver of good in them.

She grabbed my hair again and jerked me towards her. "No one out there gives a shit about you." She slammed my head against the door, crushing my nose. Blood gushed out, dripping onto my shirt. I slid down the door, tears streaming from my eyes.

"Tell me what I want to know, or I'll make this as painful as possible." She bent over and I slapped my hand against her ear. She stumbled back, holding her ear. I jumped to my feet, aiming another punch but she kicked at my stomach, slamming me back into the door and knocking the air out of me. Pain shot up my arm from my burned and blackened hand and my head throbbed. My whole body was in pain.

I wheezed in a deep breath, clutching at my stomach. Then I crawled to my knees and stumbled across the room towards the chair. Reaching it, I jumped to my feet and swiveled, slamming it against her. She fell to her side and I kicked her in the face.

Blood ran from her nose and she laughed. She fucking laughed at me.

I didn't wait to ask her why. I gripped the table, intending to slam it against her too. But she just gave me this funny look and suddenly all the oxygen was sucked from my lungs. I put my hand to my throat, trying to take a breath, and fell to my knees.

We stared at each other, both with bloody noses and damaged bodies. Her, with that fucking weird laugh and me, grasping at her, trying to force her to give me air. My nails scratched her face and she frowned, then slapped me across the face.

She stood up. "See, Lizzy. This isn't as fun." She slapped me again. "As fucking."

She took a step back, watching me as my lips turned blue. I fell to the ground, trying to crawl to her. I needed air. I needed it now.

"I don't think you're going to give me what I want." She shrugged. "That's okay, that's not the real reason you're here. My men are already searching every single room of your house. If it's not there, they have instructions to kill Riley and search Hunter's place. And then, every single safe room you guys have. I'm sure they'll find them somewhere."

The air around us glowed a bright blue and I looked up, still clasping at my throat. The necklace pulsed at her chest and I grew weaker. She was draining my own power from me. That bitch!

So I still had it. She'd managed to suppress it somehow.

"Now's the time for me to tell you why I brought you here." Her hold on my air lightened just a little and I managed to drag in a breath before she cut it off again. I crawled towards her, kneeling on her feet. She leaned over. "I just wanted to tell you I was sorry about your dad. I did regret what happened to him. I am truly sorry he had to die. He was always too trusting, too optimistic."

My power grew brighter; she was building it up. It pooled around her hand, and she smiled down at me. She was going to kill me with my own power.

"Oh, Lizzy, this feels nice. I almost wish I could keep you around a little bit longer. Just to have this amazing power you hold. Unfortunately, that won't be possible. Goodbye, little pup."

Her magic on my lungs released and I took in a sucking breath. I lunged upwards, grabbing the knife tucked in her pants, and stabbed it in her back, grunting. I screamed out. "That's for my dad, you psychopathic bitch!"

She screamed and stumbled backwards. "You whore!"

Suddenly the door slammed open. Ember swiveled, throwing my power at the person rushing inside and it slammed into Liam.

"No!" Ember cried out in shock. She stumbled towards him, the knife still lodged in her back. He fell to the ground, instantly dead. Her scream rent through the room.

Then Gerard ran in with my guys right behind him and I gasped in surprise. They were alive!

Gerard reached into his pocket and pulled out the biggest, baddest, motherfucking sword I've ever seen and sliced it through Ember's neck. Her head rolled across the floor, flinging her blood through the room, and landed with a dull thud. The blaze in the room diminished into a low fire and I instantly felt my powers again.

And then my guys were there, all surrounding me. I couldn't stop the tears as they pulled me into their arms. They were alive!

All the feelings were back, rushing into me. I felt their relief, their anger and determination to find me. Their testosterone was through the roof. They'd fought through her soldiers to get to me; I could smell blood on their clothes. The feeling made me want to punch somebody.

And then their love and happiness crushed me, flooding my senses.

I soaked it all in, every single emotion. Welcoming it, because it meant that they were alive.

Christian was holding me in his lap, and Hunter's hands were all over me, healing me. Easton had his hands in my hair, clutching my head to his chest. Then Avery pushed Easton aside and he knelt down to face me.

"Fuck, Lizzy. I was afraid we might be too late." He pulled me to him, kissing me and wrapping my arms around his neck. He opened himself up, and his emotions washed over me. They were stronger than the other guys; he felt so much! I took in a breath, sucking in precious air as he dragged me under with his feelings. Hurt, rage, despair, violence, shame, relief, and so much fucking love that it overwhelmed all the rest. It tore through my chest, burning and sealing it. He loved me so fucking much it hurt.

I kissed him, then pulled him into my arms. Needing to feel him against my chest. "Thank God you all are alive. She told me her soldiers killed you."

They all chuckled, still touching me. "They *tried* to kill us."

I smiled, so happy. Then I remembered.

"Wait, wait." I pushed them gently aside, and Avery's hand lingered on my shirt as I crawled towards Ember's headless body. My necklace was in a pool of blood around her neck. I snatched it out, then clasped it in my hand. *Mine.*

Gerard was leaning over Liam's dead body and I looked over, suddenly remembering that she'd killed him.

"Hunter! See if you can help him."

Gerard grasped my arm. "No, Lizzy. It's too late for Hunter. It needs to be you."

I hesitated and he frowned. "Hurry, before it's too late."

I gulped in a breath and closed my eyes, feeling for my power. It blossomed at my touch. I opened my eyes and scrambled to Liam's lifeless body.

"He helped us look for you. We wouldn't have found you in time if it wasn't for him."

I nodded, understanding what Gerard was trying to tell me, and put my hands over his chest. Right where my power had landed. His flesh was mangled and charred.

I took in a deep breath and my power immediately sparked and flowed through my body, as if eager to help. Focusing every intent on Liam, I directed it towards him. Rushing through me, it poured out and into his body, flooding into it like a dam had opened. Feeling it ebb and flow through me, I searched for a spark of life, anything to cling to, until I found a small white light, feeble and blinking slowly. I latched onto it, pouring everything I had into it. Sweat poured down my face and I focused with intense concentration.

I had to bring him back; I owed him my life.

My magic surrounded him and his life spark, growing stronger and brighter until it exploded. Liam shot up, sucking in a large breath and looked around the room.

His eyes landed on Ember's dead, headless body and he cried out. "No!"

Screaming, he scrambled to his knees, crawling for her, but Gerald stepped in between them. For an old dude, Gerard was surprisingly strong, and he pushed Liam back.

Feeling horrible, I stood up. The walls closed in on all sides; I had to get out of here. Christian and Avery stepped forward, leading me. Hunter and Easton took both sides of Liam, lightly pulling him, stumbling and confused, forward.

Dead soldiers met me, their bodies shot or cut up. I must have been in shock because I could only conjure a small amount of sympathy for them. For a woman who didn't like being asked to sacrifice herself for a Queen, she'd asked these men to sacrifice their lives for some old relics.

I shook my head. Psychopaths don't make sense. I just hoped they didn't have families that cared for them.

I shivered, remembering how her head flew across the room and it made me retch.

Christian and Avery put their arms around me. "Are you going to be okay?"

I nodded, folding myself into Avery. "Take me home."

He nodded, kissing the top of my head. "Always."

*I*t took us a while to get out of the tunnels and by the time we emerged into the cool air, my feet were dragging. After speaking a few words to Gerard, Hunter ran ahead of us. Liam was silent now, walking on his own.

Hunter pulled up in Easton's car a few minutes later and I sat in the back, sandwiched in between Christian and Avery.

Avery immediately pulled me into him and I settled against his chest. We were all sweaty, bloody and gross, but we were freaking together again. Avery's emotions buzzed between him and me, warm and welcoming, tender and concerned. I glowered in them. They moved over me, bathing me in his warmth and love.

Christian leaned towards me, brushing his thumb against my cheek. I smiled and took his hand. He scooted closer and he leaned against me. We held hands as Hunter pulled out in to the street.

Avery's voice was by my ear. "Are you okay?" His fingers lightly stroked my stomach.

I was surrounded by men who loved me. Who risked their lives to find me.

I was lucky.

I nodded. "Yeah. That bitch is dead, so I'm feeling pretty good right now."

He chuckled softly, and then silence settled around us. No one spoke as we drove home, and I inspected my guys. They had cuts and bruises, and their hair was messy, but no real wounds. They looked exhausted. They'd been fighting, just like I had, and we were all ready to fall into a dream coma.

I tried to stay awake but my eyes grew heavy and I dozed.

I awoke to Hunter's voice. "Go check and come back." A car door slammed and I opened my eyes and leaned forward. "Are we there yet?"

Avery's hand tightened on my stomach, pulling me back into him. "Not yet. Are you hungry?"

I shook my head.

"Alright, go back to sleep."

"Okay." I wouldn't argue against that. Nodding, I snuggled closer into him and fell back asleep.

I awoke again, shivering lightly.

"Lizzy, I need your help." Easton was standing in the door, his hand held out to me. I grabbed it and he pulled me out of the car. Then he picked me up into his arms, cradling me as we walked up to the house.

I looked up at it. "Wait. That's not our house."

His lips pressed into a thin line. "They ransacked our place, so we're staying here for now."

Yawning, I wrapped my hands around his neck and settled against his shoulder in a sleepy daze. "Alright." I had my necklace and my guys. That was all I really cared about.

Christian jogged ahead of us and I didn't notice much as Easton took me inside. He set me down and I looked around. I was in the bathroom and the shower was on.

"Shower. Here's some clean clothes." Christian put a towel and some clothes on a shelf next to the shower. "You can sleep in the bed out there." He pointed to the bed behind in the adjoining room.

I nodded. "Thanks."

He smiled and then him and Easton left, shutting the door behind them.

At the click of the door, I jerked awake, alone with my memories.

I wrapped my arms around my chest, shaking. Fuck, that woman was so disgusting. So deranged.

I tested the water; it was deliciously warm. I jumped inside, grabbing a bar of soap. I needed to clean her filth off my body. I scrubbed every crook and cranny, once, twice, three times. Until I couldn't smell anything of her or that dungeon on my body.

The warm water was like a lullaby, and I grew sleepy again. Barely keeping my eyes open, I climbed out of the shower. My uniform was on the floor. I could smell her blood on them and my own desire. I began to retch again and I leaned over the toilet, dry heaving.

After making sure I was done, I turned on the sink and splashed my face with cool water and rinsed out my mouth. That's when I noticed the bottled water next to the sink.

Someone must have slipped it in here while I was showering. I smiled, thumbing the plastic. I opened the lid and drank the whole bottle, grateful for the men in my life.

I threw my clothes in the trash. I couldn't look at them. I certainly wasn't going to wear them again. After drying off, I shrugged into Christian's clothes, then collapsed in the bed, falling asleep.

§

SUNLIGHT POURED THROUGH THE WINDOW AND I WAS IN A VERY COMFY bed, sweating. Christian's arm clung to my stomach, and I found the heat source. His arm was pulsing shots of warmth into my body, even while he slept.

I stared at him in awe. I had the feeling that Christian's need to heal went to the very core of his essence. He was so connected to his power, that it acted out his needs without him even knowing it.

Even though I was hot, it was still soothing. I flung the blanket off my legs but snuggled closer and faced him. He snored lightly and I stared at his angelic face. His blond hair curled around his eyes, framing his long eyelashes. He looked so sweet, so sexy.

I brushed my fingers over his lips, softly so he wouldn't wake, and a breathtaking love for him clung to my heart, making it pound softly against my chest. I kissed his cheek lightly, then I slowly crawled out from under his arm and quietly made my way to the bathroom.

I looked at myself in the mirror. My hair was a mess but the rest of my body had been perfectly healed by Hunter. Looking around, I found a toothbrush and toothpaste. I brushed my teeth and took a quick rinse in the shower. Then I put my clothes back on and took off my necklace.

After carefully sliding the diamond off, I studied the chain. It was discolored from Ember's blood.

Turning on the water, I rinsed it off, rubbing my fingers over it. When that didn't do anything, I pumped soap into my hand and scrubbed it. I spent several minutes scrubbing it but the blood wouldn't come off. Instead the chain grew even more discolored, turning a rusty, brownish color. Frustrated, I put the diamond back on it and secured it around my neck. There must be something magical about her blood that didn't quit even though she was dead.

Sighing, I put it back on, forcing myself to shrug it off. I'd just have to get another chain. I was tempted to cling to it; my mom had given it to me. But the diamond was the most important part. I washed my hands again and turned back to the room, realizing that Christian was watching me.

My lips broke out in a grin. "You're awake." I went back to the bed.

He smiled. "Hey, beautiful." His green eyes darkened. "How are you doing?"

I shrugged. "I'm okay." I sat down, pulling my legs up and wrapping my arms around them. "How are you?"

"Me? I'm doing great." He leaned over and drug me to him. "Now that you're back."

I smiled, and a glowy warmth moved through my chest. As I settled back under the covers, he frowned.

"What? Why the frown?" I touched his lips and he nipped at my finger. "Do I still have bad breath?"

He shook his head. "Nope."

"Then what?"

Shrugging, he didn't answer but scooted up so that his back was against the grey, padded headboard. He pulled me up so that I was leaning against his chest, and he ran his fingers over my head, playing with my hair. He didn't have a shirt on and I ran my fingers through the light blonde hair on his chest, thinking. Remembering.

I could hear the birds chirping outside our window and the voice of Hunter, Easton and Avery outside. It sounded like they were playing soccer.

"The guys are up already?"

He turned his head, glancing at the clock. "It's already two in the afternoon, so probably." Then he shrugged. "But I don't know. I've been in here with you all night."

A smile touched my lips. "Thank you."

"For what?"

"For being with me. For keeping me safe. For coming for me."

He didn't answer right away, and his fingers through my hair were lulling me into a peaceful calm feeling.

"What did she want anyway?" His voice was thoughtful.

"To know where the book and the ring were."

"Mmmm."

"I didn't tell her."

His hands traced my ear. "It doesn't matter. We've given them back to Gerard. Along with the mask and the astrolabe. They found them on one of the bodies of her dead guards."

"Good." I shivered, but I still felt a weight lift off my chest. "They should keep them safe now."

"Yeah."

"How did you find me? How did you know to go to Liam?"

His fingers traced down my neck. "It was Sophia."

I sat up, my eyes wide. "Really?"

He nodded. "She went through Andre's personal computer at his home. She found evidence that it had some sort of unauthorized program on it. It kept a log of keystrokes, stuff like that. She traced it to Ember. Apparently, Andre suspected that the Queen had a mole, and was doing his own investigation. He only worked on it from his personal laptop, in case it was someone inside the Authority. Ember knew everything he was doing. Knew that he was close to discovering her identity. She's the one who threw suspicion on him, to keep the Queen from trusting him. That way, even if he came out and said that it was Ember, they wouldn't believe him."

I raised my eyebrows, still surprised that Sophia was the shifter responsible for saving us. "Hmm."

"Once she knew it was Ember, she tried calling us. When she couldn't reach us, she called Andre and told him the truth. Liam helped them track her closest known associates. With Gerard's help, they split up, looking for her. And us." He frowned, remembering, "We woke up as Ember's soldiers were dragging us to the river. They were going to kill us and dump us in the water. We were fighting them off, but there were so many." He looked into my eyes, his stare intense. "Liam and Gerard came just in time."

"Thank God." I breathed a sigh of relief. "And um, that sword Gerard pulled out of his pocket? What the hell?"

Christian laughed. "Yeah, the sword breaks any magical elements. So if Ember had any magic protecting her, it would've destroyed it the minute his sword touched her."

I frowned. "Remind me not to get in a fight with him."

He smiled, crinkling the skin around his eyes. "Nah, he likes you too much."

I smiled. "I hope so. I've saved the Queen's ass too many times for him to hold any sort of grudge against me. He owes me for the rest of my life." I paused, and my smile slipped from my face. "You know, Ember told me that she manipulated Andre into banishing Emma from Aerwyna."

His eyebrows shot up. "Really?"

I nodded. "Yeah."

"That would be really hard, I can't imagine anyone manipulating

Andre. He doesn't have enough feelings to be controlled. She must have something over him."

I frowned. "I think I know how."

Christian tilted his head. "How's that?"

I didn't answer, just looked out the window. The snow was almost gone, and the blazing sun was doing its best to melt the rest.

Christian touched my chin and I looked at him. "Christian?"

He gave me a soft look. "Yes?"

I sat up, pulling my knees up and lying my chin on it. I took his hand and played with his fingers, uncertain how to ask him my question. "Have you, erm…" I paused, trying to stop the squeezing feeling in my chest. A warmth moved through Christian's fingers and into my arms, and the feeling loosened. I sucked in a breath, feeling better. Swallowing hard, I stared at the white down blanket.

"Have you, uh… Have you ever heard of any magical powers that dragons can have…" I glanced at him then back at the blanket. "Sexual powers?" I blushed.

He gently pulled my chin up to look him in the eyes.

"Yes, I have heard of that."

"And, and… how does it work? Does the… recipient have any… any control over their feelings?"

He shook his head. "No."

I bit my lip, trying to hold back the tears that threatened to spill from my eyes. He looked into my eyes, a fierce look on his face. "Elizabeth, you are not at fault for anything that happened there."

Suddenly, tears were streaming down my face and I was sucking in the sobs that threatened to spill out. He pulled me into his arms, rocking me gently and I lost myself in him, his kindness, his love.

I was surprised by my emotions. I didn't realize how I was really feeling until now. Angry and so… So violated. But his touch, his concern, his everything made me feel like I was okay, everything would be fine.

I pulled up and took in his face, the troubled look in his eyes, the straight nose, and the heavenly scent that I came to know as Christian. I kissed him, pulling his jaw forward to deepen the kiss. His hands went to my shoulders, holding them tight, then he slowly pushed me away, breaking the kiss and I looked up at him.

"Are you sure this is what you want, Pinky?"

I nodded. "Yes. This is what I want." I was sure of it. I was a fighter. And I wasn't going to let anything she did stop me from enjoying every single bit of life. "I want you to erase everything she did from my body."

He began to kiss me and climbed out from under the covers. His lips caressed mine as he pulled me closer. And then he sat up, kneeling across from me, staring into my eyes. Reaching down, he slowly pulled up my shirt. I held up my arms and he drug it over my head, flinging it to the floor. I felt a sudden sense of relief. Like he'd just taken away my pain with the flick of his wrist.

His eyes slowly took me in, betraying his desire. "You are so sexy."

I burned inside. Burned with his smoldering eyes on me, his sexy lips itching to touch me, burned with feeling for him. The heat rose as he took my hand, placing soft kisses up my arm.

His lips were warm and his healing power slowly seared up into my arm. He moved higher, to my shoulder and up my neck, then down to my chest. Each touch of his lips burned and scalded my insides, burning through Ember's hate and manipulation and lust. Burning her from my mind.

He moved slowly, and even though my whole body was on fire, he didn't miss a single inch of my skin, my pain, my heartache. His teeth grazed the bottom of my feet and up to my ankles. The heat stirred hotter as his lips moved up my thighs.

I groaned as his fingers tugged my shorts off. I opened my legs, giving him everything of me, baring myself completely, as his pulsing warm healing powers ran up my leg into my core. I was so wet, so needy, so hot for his thick dick inside me. I closed my eyes, squirming and pressing my chest forward as his tongue made its way up my inner thigh to the vee of my legs.

He paused and I looked up at him. He was staring at my pussy like it was the most beautiful thing he'd ever seen. Then his tongue snaked out and he licked my clit, just once. He kissed it tenderly and everything in me felt whole and clean, so fucking taken care of and loved. And so fucking ready for him. His loving touches lit my whole body, igniting it until it was a blazing, raging need for him.

I moaned, sitting up to taste his wet mouth, to lean into him, into his strong hands that were lovingly caressing and exploring. I ran my fingers down his chest to the top of his sweats and swiped my finger in the curly hair snaking out of the top. And then I hooked my fingers on the top of his pants and pulled it down. His erection sprung out and I grasped his hardness in my hand, stroking it softly.

"Shit, Lizzy." His lips pressed into mine again, devouring me like a man who hadn't had a drink for weeks. His hands gripped my jaw, and he pressed his chest into me. My whole body responded to his passion. I ground myself against him, moaning his name. Needing him inside me, needing his love to fill me up.

But first, I wanted him on my lips, to show how much I fucking loved him.

I leaned forward, pushing him. He fell onto his back and I pulled his legs out from under him, yanking off his sweats. I stared in awe at his sexy body as he stretched out across the bed, his dick an open invitation. Climbing in between his legs, I stroked his thickness.

"You like this?"

He nodded, groaning, and his arms went over his head, clutching at the sheets. I watched him as I stroked, loving the look on his face, loving that I was turning him on. Then I leaned down and swirled my tongue around the head. He sucked in a deep breath and I smiled, grasping the base with my hand. I moved my mouth slowly, deliberately, down his shaft.

He thrust forward, clasping my head to him and I took him in all the way to the back of my throat. Then I pulled back to the tip, swirling my tongue while my hands milked his cock. He groaned again, making sexy growling noises in the back of his throat as I moved up and down over him. I spread my legs wider, sinking deeper, sucking harder and faster. I needed him inside me.

"Shit, Lizzy." He grasped my hand, arching his back, bucking his hips into me as I fell into him, claiming him with my mouth, my heart, with breathless gasps. I relished in the power I had over him and my necklace pulsed at my chest, bathing us in her warm power.

Suddenly, his hand was on my head, stopping me. "Fuck, fuck, I can't take any..." He sat up, jerking me forward and I fell onto his chest. His eyes stared into mine. His voice was deep and sexy. "Are you sure you're okay?"

"Yes." I nodded, frowning, upset that he didn't let me finish. "And If you don't stop treating me like I'm going to break, I'll—"

Growling, he didn't let me finish my sentence. In one motion he flipped me on my stomach, pinning me to the bed. Then he yanked on my hips, pulling my ass up into the air. My face mashed into the bed as he pulled my hands behind my back. He reached over me and I heard the side drawer open. A silky material threaded around my wrists and he pulled them together in a smooth, threading motion, tying them behind my back.

I was vulnerable and exposed.

He leaned over me again, his voice harsh and biting as he wrapped one hand lightly around my throat, rubbing his hard dick against my side. "I'm going to fuck you so hard, you're going to think I hate your pussy. Now, spread your legs for me, Pinky." He yanked my legs apart and they strained to keep me upright as his hands ran up my inner thigh.

Fuck.

I moaned, twisting my hips as shooting pain slowly traveled up and into the softness of my vulva. I cried out, coming undone at his touch, panting with need.

"Yes, Christian. More."

"Is this what you do want? You don't want me to treat you like a poor, broken, kitten?"

"Yes." I moaned into the bed, straining at the ties at my wrists. Then his hand came down across my ass, striking it. I cried out, then strained to push it out higher. More. He bit it, then rubbed his nose across it, licking and biting, spreading my legs wider to slide his finger between my lips harshly.

I rubbed myself against his hand; my juices pooled in his fingers, running down my thighs and his wrists. I was leaking with want and need as his fingers expertly played with me. My mouth fell open and I bit the blanket as pleasure and pain from his power bit into my pussy.

Then he pulled me back up onto my knees, thrusting my chest forward with my hands still behind my back. He wrapped his hands in my hair, tugging my head to the side to expose my neck.

"Fuck, Pinky. I want you so bad." His hand came up to my neck, splaying his fingers over it. Then he scraped his teeth across my jaw. "Ever since I saw your sad, sexy face, I wanted you in my bed, under me, my cock jutting and fucking you."

"Yes." I panted. "Fuck me, Christian."

His hand came up to my nipple, pinching it and sending a shot of electricity through me. "I'll fuck you when I'm good and ready."

I leaned into him, staring into his eyes. "That's right, Christian. You'll fuck me when you're ready. But you're going to fuck me harder and deeper and faster than you've ever fucked anyone before. Make me scream your name."

Growling, he pushed me back onto the bed. My hands were still tied behind my back and he leaned over me, not touching me. His green eyes were so dark and intense, staring into the soul of my Alpha. Daring me to come out and play. I growled, lifting my head to bite his lip.

Blood dripped into my mouth and I licked it, still staring into his eyes. "Make me scream, Christian."

Growling, he pushed his thumbs into my hips, pressing me into the bed so that my breasts pushed out and my nipples' tips pebbled in the cool air. He dug his knee up into my cunt, spreading my thighs. And then my body was open and pressing outward, completely on display for him.

"You're like fucking dessert, spread out for me like this." His cock, hard and firm, pressed against my thigh. "God, you're sexy." He moaned, submitting to his temptation, and rammed his dick into my soft folds. I was dripping with want, so tight on the edge of the precipice of loosing it, and he slid in and out easily, harshly, clinging to me. Then his hands wrapped behind my back, pulling and yanking until my wrists were free.

Everything inside me threatened to bust. The necklace at my neck was hot and blue magic shot out and into the room. I gripped onto his shoulders and wrapped my ankles around his back. I dug my heels into his back, thrusting my hips to force him deeper into me. I closed my eyes as he pounded into me; all I could do was love and feel and fuck and take him into me, the big fucking dragon that he was.

"Yes," my voice came out desperate and needy. "More, harder."

He slammed into me harder, his pubic bone slamming against my clit. Every hit of his bone against my clit sent me high, higher and I was so close, so high. He pulled my hands up, pinning them over my head as he fucked me, pulling my knee to my chest, spreading me wider for his dick. Panting and puffing, I shifted my hips to urge him faster, deeper, harder.

Then his thumb, warm and silky, dug into the soft flesh of my clit and my hips jerked forward, as a wave of lust ripped over me. His thumb dug in harder, scraping against my clit with no forgiveness, no absolution, just fucking me with his cock and his thumb harsher and faster. "Yes, fuck, Christian, yes!" Wave upon wave of pleasure washed over me, shredding me to pieces.

And then his cum shot up into me, filling all the missing pieces of my body, my heart, my mind and I jerked one more time, letting a soft orgasm roll through me.

He fell into me and I wrapped my hands around his back, his breathing harsh. His hands gripped me tight, like he never wanted to let go. I trailed my fingers down his back, feeling his warm breath over my shoulder.

"Fuck, Christian. That was amazing."

He tilted his head to nip my ear. "You liked it?"

I nodded, whispering. "Yes."

I pressed my palms into his back, holding him close to my chest. We lay like that for a moment, feeling, touching, loving, being.

"Lizzy."

I looked at him.

"I love you. I'm glad we're sharing. It feels right."

A wave of warmth and love overwhelmed me. Fuck, Christian just gave and gave and it made me feel so fucking wanted and loved.

I hugged him close. "I love you, babe." I rubbed my cheek against his. "I fucking love you."

We lay on the bed like that for a while, listening to the sounds of the birds and the guys playing soccer. Their playful banter was a soothing balm to my soul, happy that everyone was getting along.

"Do you feel any better?" His voice rumbled through his chest and it made me shiver.

I nodded, even though his eyes were closed. "Mhmm."

"Good." His finger circled my nipple and it perked for him. "I'm glad. Did you want to talk about it?"

I closed my eyes, joining him in the darkness to focus my thoughts on the attention he was giving my nipple. "Not really."

I felt him nod against my breast. "Okay." We fell into the quiet, each lost in our thoughts. I felt his breathing, slow and steady on my chest. He was probably lost in his thoughts but his finger was still flicking my nipple and I was starting to come alive again. Then he rolled it in between his fingers and a moan slipped out.

I opened my eyes, staring at him lazily. He was looking up at me, a smirk on his face.

I smiled, pressing my chest out. "I love it when you play with my nipples."

He grinned and flicked it again. "Like this?"

I nodded, biting my lip. "Yes, like that."

Giving me a mischievous grin, he leaned down and bit the tip. "Like this?"

Growling, I flipped him over onto his back, straddling him. I rubbed myself against him, sliding over his slick body. "You want more?" I moved down, sliding myself over his budding erection. "You want my pussy again?"

He sat up, pulling me to him as my hips moved over him. His gaze betrayed his desire, his words a plea in my ear. "I'll always want you, Lizzy."

I PULLED A BOTTLED WATER OUT OF THE FRIDGE, HANDING ONE TO Christian.

He grinned, thanking me, and the soft and sweet dragon was back. I stepped into him, nuzzling his neck and his fingers traced my back.

"Where'd the rest of the guys go?"

The house and yard were empty. He shrugged, then tipped his water bottle and I watched his lips as he cupped the lid, drinking. I shivered, remembering those lips on me and then leaned back over the fridge, grabbing another one.

Just as I finished gulping down the whole bottle, the front door opened. Avery, Hunter and Easton rushed inside, holding bags of groceries. They were laughing and immediately the house felt full, happy.

I threw my bottle in the recycling, then ran to help them.

Avery handed me two bags, smirking at me. "Good to see you leave your room, squirt."

I rolled my eyes, smiling. "Jealous?" I teased him.

He leaned over and, wrapping his hand around my jaw, kissed me. I couldn't touch him, wrap my arms around him like I wanted to, so I just leaned into the kiss. Then he pulled back, staring into my eyes. Reaching up, he pinched my cheek. "Maybe." Grinning, he walked back towards the front door to grab more groceries.

"I haven't forgotten you owe us dinner!" I call out to him.

He waved a hand at me before walking out the door. "Got it!"

I smiled, then turned back around, feeling just so damn lucky to have a houseful of sexy, amazing, and considerate men. Hunter was putting food in the fridge and I took a moment to appreciate his fine ass. Then I walked to the counter to unload my bags.

"Here, let me show you where things go." Easton stepped up next to me, opening the cupboards to help. Avery came back inside with the last of the groceries and began to pull out mixing bowls and pans.

When everything was put away, Easton grabbed my hand. "Let me show you the house."

I grinned as he tugged me into the living room. From what I remembered from last night, the outside of the house looked like a French villa, with front gardens that were just starting to sprout little plants. The inside was large and sprawling, and it took us a while to go through it. I clutched Easton's hand as he showed me the living room that had several skylights and was decorated with antique French furniture. The French resemblance ended after that, though, and he led me through the hallway, pointing out everyone's rooms. My guys all had their own, and they were decorated according to their own taste. There were also several spare bedrooms, a billiard room, and a bowling alley.

Then he drug me outside. There was a pool and a jacuzzi, and an empty field where I assumed they were playing soccer earlier. When I saw the pool, I shook my head. "Now, why the hell didn't we stay here earlier?"

He turned to me, grinning. "Cuz the gym is small, and it's in the basement. It's doable for the basics but not very nice. And you were in training, remember?"

I smiled, remembering. "Yeah."

"But we'll have to use that gym now, because we're staying here for a few days, maybe even longer. Until they figure out what to do with us. In the meantime, I'm going to just relax and enjoy myself." His eyes darkened. "And I can think of several ways to enjoy you, too, now that you've officially asked us to share."

My eyebrows rose. "Oh, really?"

He grinned. "Yeah, really." He wrapped his arms around me. I lifted my face to him, ready for a kiss, but instead he picked me up and dropped me in the pool.

I froze as I slipped underwater. The water was cold! I pushed off the bottom and broke out of the water, yelling. "You bastard! It's freezing!"

He jumped in beside me, and when he broke the surface, he was grinning. I splashed water at him. "Thanks a lot."

Growling, he grabbed my hand, glancing at my tits that were nice and perky and showing plainly through Christian's white t-shirt. He pushed me back into the wall, nuzzling my neck. Suddenly, I wasn't as cold anymore. His tongue snaked out, sampling the pool water off my neck. "Now this is more what I had in mind." He gripped me to him, moving his thumbs over the tips of my breasts and I fell into him, surrendering. "Be prepared Lizzy, because we're all hungry for you. And we plan on fucking you into oblivion these next few days, each one taking turns until we're all satisfied."

I leaned against him, nodding. "Okay." I couldn't say no. I didn't want to.

His fingers lowered, playing with the tie to my sweats. "Ever had sex in the pool, Lizzy?"

There was loud, roaring noise and Avery, Christian, and Hunter rushed to the pool. I looked up in time to see them jump in. I laughed at Avery's large smile as he curled into a ball before hitting the water.

Easton grunted, pressing me into him. "We'll finish this later." He growled this in my ear before letting me go. Hunter swam up to me, his eyebrows wiggling.

"What you guys doing?"

Easton frowned and turned to him. "You know what we were doing."

Hunter grinned and pulled me to him, cradling me in between his legs as he leaned against the side of the pool. "I'm pretty sure it's Avery's turn."

I frowned, looking at Avery who was racing Christian to the other end of the pool. "I think Avery's going to have to wait."

"Why?"

I ran my hand through my hair, pulling stray pieces out of my eye. "Avery and I need to work on our trust, first."

Easton grinned, laughing. "Oh, he's going to hate that."

I smiled back at him. "I know."

Hunter chuckled and I leaned into him, settling myself as his thumb traced my stomach. We turned to watch Christian touch the end of the pool right before Avery. Making a triumphant noise, Christian threw his hands into the air but Avery jumped on him, dragging him under the water. After struggling for a minute, Avery and Christian both came up for air, grinning and walking towards us.

Avery wrapped his hands across his chest. "It's cold. Who wants to get in the jacuzzi? I turned it on earlier." His smile was catching and I stood up, feeling happy.

"I'll join you." He grabbed my hand, leading me and everyone else, out. We rushed across the red bricks towards the jacuzzi. Christian's sweats clung to my hips, threatening to drop to the ground, so I slid them off and jumped in the water in my underwear and t-shirt.

"Mmm…" The water was so warm. I instantly relaxed as the warm water hit my legs and I glanced at Christian, remembering the last time we were in the jacuzzi together.

He gave me a small smile and I settled next to Avery in the jacuzzi. Hunter claimed the other spot next to me.

"So," Christian turned on the bubbles. "What do you think is going to happen next?"

Easton sat across from me, looking at Christian. "We're going to get dressed and choke down Avery's food." Avery splashed water at him. "Then watch a movie. And just take a few days off, taking turns with Princess over there," Easton nodded at me, "except for Avery, of course."

Easton glanced at me, giving me a knowing grin that slipped away as soon as Christian faced him.

Avery's face turned red and Christian slammed his fist against Easton's shoulder. "Don't talk like that."

He gave Christian a snarky look. "It's okay, I've already confirmed it with her."

"Hey, what the hell?" Avery looked at me and I just shrugged. He tried to slip his hand out of mine, but I gripped it tighter, stroking my thumb against his palm. I pulled him closer, then turned to straddle his lap, ignoring the lecture Christian was giving Easton. "I think you have some work to do before you get a taste of this." My voice was soft, so no one could hear me but us. "You need to prove to me that you can earn my fuck."

His dick bulged in his shorts and he pulled me a little closer, stroking my sides.

"Oh, yeah?"

I nodded.

"And what kind of things am I going to have to do to taste that sweet cunt of yours?"

His dirty words were turning me on but I leaned forward to whisper in his ear, smirking. "You can start off by fixing us dinner, every night this week."

He groaned, running his free hand through his beard. "Fine." He looked back at me, and his eyes were dark. "Only if I get to eat it off you."

I melted at his words. "Depends on what you make. What'd you cook tonight?"

He choked on his words. "I didn't plan for that tonight."

I laughed. "Okay, seriously, wha'd you make? I need to know if I should really enforce this." I leaned forward, pressing my hands on his shoulders. "Are you a good cook?"

"Does that mean if I make horrible food I'll get out of this arrangement?"

I shook my head. "Nope. It just means I eat a few snacks before dinner."

He grinned, "I can cook if I want. I made chicken and eggplant parmigiana. It's in the oven. And Hunter made a salad."

I raised my eyebrows, impressed. "And what are you cooking tomorrow?"

He sighed. "You're serious about this, aren't you?"

I shook my head. "Absolutely. How many meals did I have to cook in Hawaii?"

His lips turned up into a smile. "Yeah, that was pretty nice, having a woman look after me."

I smiled, feeling all glowy and squishy inside. I ran my hand through his beard, tugging it softly. "Thanks for not shaving."

His smile turned into a grin. "You really like it?"

I nodded. "I love it."

"Good. Then I'll keep it." He leaned forward, kissing me softly. When he pulled away, I traced my fingers over his tattoo of the unicorn.

"Listen, I'm sorry about Mia. I know you loved her and..." I looked into his eyes. "I promise I'll try not to end up like her." It wasn't eloquent, but I wanted him to feel that he was safe opening his heart to me.

He breathed in deeply. "I think we'll be okay. You were right. I think together, we'll make it." He looked behind me and I turned. Hunter and Christian were laughing, then Easton splashed water at Hunter, a grumpy look on Easton's face.

"I agree." Smiling, I nodded and he nuzzled my neck.

Christian's words cut through our conversation. "Anyway, back to what I was talking about before. I meant the Queen. Liam and Andre. Any news on what's happening now?"

I turned back around, still sitting in Avery's lap.

"I think they're going to do a full investigation into Liam."

"They might need to do one on Andre." Christian's eyes bore into me and all eyes turned to me. Avery put his arm around me, stroking the side of my stomach.

"I think that Ember's been using Andre. She had a very persuasive personality." I didn't go into further details.

Hunter bit his lip, thinking. "Okay, I'll let them know."

"What about Sophia's office? Ember was able to get in at least one unsanctioned hit that we know of. There could be more."

I frowned, thinking about the people she may have killed.

Hunter tugged his bangs out of his face, sighing. "This is a shit-storm. At least they're finding the relics."

"They are?" I sat up.

Hunter nodded. "Yeah, I spoke to Edward earlier. They've rounded up a bunch of Ember's men. One of them gave up the location of her hideout."

I leaned back against Avery, relieved. "Good."

"Thanks to us." Easton was grinning and his words sparked a smile between all the guys. I didn't smile, I couldn't forget the price to Aria.

One of her best friends betrayed her. And Liam, he must be devastated.

A light blinked, then a musical melody rung through the air. All my guys except Avery stood up, a frown on their faces.

I looked around. "What's that?"

Hunter climbed out of the jacuzzi. "It's the front door. I'll get it."

Avery stood up next, pushing me off his lap but taking my hand. "Let's go check the oven."

"Good idea." We followed Hunter up the stairs.

Leaving Easton in the jacuzzi by himself, Christian walked up behind us, "I'll pick out a movie."

I glanced back at Easton. He didn't move; he just stared off towards the field with a thoughtful look on his face.

We walked towards the house and I skipped ahead of the guys, pulling my shirt off and throwing it to the ground. I heard several groans and I grinned, entering the warm house.

❧

I went to Christian's room to find dry clothes. When I leaned over, I bumped into someone.

Turning around, it was Christian. He'd snuck in so quietly, I hadn't heard him.

He had a needy look on his face which only lit the fire inside me. Pulling me to him, he kissed me softly. I opened my lips, letting his silky tongue slide against mine. His hand went to my breast, stroking the side softly, then he pulled away, brushing my hair from my face.

I smiled, biting my lip and he bent over, pulling out another drawer. "I figured you needed clothes. Shirts are here." He pulled out a black tank top and glanced at my bare chest, grinning. "Sorry, I don't have any extra bras."

I smiled. "You sure?"

He shoved that drawer closed and then opened another one, rummaging through it while I put on the tank top. It was a little big and it showed some cleavage, but not too much. He threw a pair of

171

boxers at me. "You can wear these. Tomorrow we'll go get your stuff from the other place."

"Thanks." I pulled them on and they hung on my hips.

"Looking good." He smacked my ass.

I yelped, jumping, and then a shadow filled the doorway. Hunter had a tight smile on his face.

"It's the Queen. She's here to see you. She's waiting in the living room." He looked me over. "I advise you wear something a little more covering." He raised one eyebrow. "Although later on I wouldn't mind cuddling up with you on the couch in that. I just might find a little space for my fingers to sneak in somewhere."

My face turned red and I took in a deep breath, suddenly unsure if I was ready for all the hormones that were running through my body. Living and fucking all these guys in one house was going to be mad.

He chuckled. "Don't worry, Princess. We'll take it easy, if that's what you need." He glanced out of the room. "But I would suggest you hurry, don't want to keep her waiting."

He didn't move away though, he just stood there with his hand in his pocket, looking at me like he wanted to tell me something.

"Just spit it out." I smiled at him. "I know you want to tell me something."

He stepped into the room and took my hand. Then he pulled his hand out of his pocket and placed something in my palm. I looked down; it was a beautiful silver necklace.

He eyed the one at my chest. "I didn't know if you wanted to keep that one. I know your mom gave it to you." He shrugged his shoulders and shoved his hands back into his pocket. "But I thought with the blood and all that, you might want a new one."

I looked down at it. It looked very similar to the one my mother gave me. "How did you know?"

He just shrugged and smiled mysteriously, then glanced back at Christian.

I turned around. "Did you have anything to do with this?"

Christian shook his head, but I could tell that he was lying so I gave him a look. He scowled and gave Hunter a look. Reaching out, I pulled them both to me, feeling their love pressing into me.

"Thanks, guys." I wanted to cry, I was so overcome with emotion but I held my tears in. "This means everything to me."

Hunter kissed my cheek. "You're welcome, Princess."

Giving me a tug, he smiled, then walked out the door. I turned to Christian and slapped his arm playfully. "Liar."

He grinned. "Yep, that's me."

Both Christian and I changed quickly, putting on clothes more appropriate for a Queen and fixing my necklace, then we walked out together, with him holding my hand. He led me to the living room where the Queen was sitting on the edge of a green velvet couch. She stood when we entered the room and held her arms out to me.

Her eyes were puffy and her mascara was smudged. Instead of greeting her, Christian squeezed my hand and walked off towards the kitchen. I pulled Aria into my arms and she grasped me tight. Her body was shaking but she wasn't crying, though I know she was trying not to. There were two guards near the front door and two at the back, but they didn't look at us.

After a while, she pulled back and I tugged her back on the couch. She was wearing sweatpants and a t-shirt, and she looked so strange in such casual clothes. She rubbed her red nose, taking in a deep breath and I gave her a moment to gain her composure.

"I came here to thank you, and your team, for everything you've done for me." She paused and I took her hand, gripping it softly. The dark circles under her eyes hinted that she hadn't slept in a couple of days. She opened her mouth like she wanted to say more but shut it with a snap, biting her lip like she was trying to keep her tears from falling.

"It's okay. I understand. You don't have to say anything else."

She shook her head. "No, no. I want to apologize for everything Ember put you and your team through. I know you've been through some shit. And I am sorry for it."

I tried to reassure her, I certainly didn't want her worrying about me right now. She had so much other stuff to work out. "It's fine.

Everything is good. I'm just worried about you. How are you doing with all this?"

She sucked in a breath and by the look on her face, I don't think anyone had asked her this. She stared off into the glass wall for a moment. "It's actually, a pretty bad shock." She looked at me. "Did she tell you why?"

I took a second to consider my answer. I bit my tongue and shook my head. "I just think that they got to her, you know?" Right now she didn't need to know how bitter Ember really was. Some things just don't need to be revealed. Ember's reasons wouldn't help her with the aftermath.

She nodded, knowing that I was lying, but she accepted it. "Do you know anything about them? The people she was working with?"

"Not really. She only said that they were connected to the men who killed my dad."

"I see." She nodded. "It's as we suspected, then."

I nodded with her, not knowing what else to say and silence settled between us. My hand was still on hers and I wished I had Christian's power to help heal her heart a little. I thought of offering it but then I decided against it. It might be too weird, and maybe she would feel awkward turning me down. I'd let Christian offer it himself if it was appropriate.

"Do you want to stay and eat? We're having eggplant." I said this like I wasn't sure it was going to be good or not.

She looked amused. "I'm not here to stay. I came to give you a new assignment."

I took in a deep breath, hoping she'd at least give us a few days to relax.

She smiled, nodding to one of her guards. He nodded back, then walked out the front door. "Don't worry, you'll have a couple of weeks off, if you decide that's what you need."

I gripped her hand, thanking her without saying a word.

"When you're ready, I'd like to send you home."

I sucked in a breath, as squirmy worms overtook my stomach. Gratitude overwhelmed me, and the need to go come called me like a siren. But I couldn't help the anxious feeling that cut off my breath, the way my heart pounded in my chest.

What will I find there?

She continued. "Based on what you just told me, we need more information about the people who killed your parents. And, honestly, we need them taken down." She looked into my eyes. "You need to take them down."

I nodded, gripping her hand harder. Yes. I was going to take them down.

"I know that you are, mostly, ready to go home. You've been loyal and I'm grateful for it. You have given me a great gift. However, I fear that if I don't let you return soon, you might wish you'd never declared fealty to me." She tried to grin, teasing me a little, but it only came across as a sad smile.

"Thank you." It was all I could think of to say.

"But. I do hope to see you again, one day."

I pulled her into my arms, hugging her tight. "Of course."

She held me for a moment and the bond between us strengthened. I would definitely keep in touch. Then she took in a breath, pulling back. "And, erm, I know that I've already asked so much of you but there is one thing left for you to take care of."

The door opened and I heard Hunter's voice growl from the kitchen. "Oh, hell no."

I looked over and saw the guard returning with James, who gave Hunter the biggest eat-shit grin.

"What's up, guys?"

PLEASE

Note from the Author:

Order the next book here.

Tell the world how you feel about this book. Write a review! You would immediately own my heart forever!!!

Thank you!

Made in the USA
Columbia, SC
08 November 2018